BECAUSE THE EARL LOVED ME

HAPPILY EVER AFTER BOOK 6

ELLIE ST. CLAIR

CONTENTS

Chapter 1	1
Chapter 2	9
Chapter 3	18
Chapter 4	25
Chapter 5	33
Chapter 6	41
Chapter 7	50
Chapter 8	59
Chapter 9	67
Chapter 10	75
Chapter 11	82
Chapter 12	90
Chapter 13	97
Chapter 14	105
Chapter 15	113
Chapter 16	121
Chapter 17	129
Chapter 18	137
Chapter 19	145
Chapter 20	154
Chapter 21	161
Chapter 22	169
Chapter 23	179
Chapter 24	185
Chapter 25	191
Chapter 26	198
Chapter 27	205
Chapter 28	213
Epilogue	220
An excerpt from Quest of Honor	225
Also by Ellie St. Clair	233
About the Author	237

♥ **Copyright 2018 by Ellie St Clair**

All rights reserved.

This book or parts thereof may not be reproduced in any form, stored in any retrieval system, or transmitted in any form by any means—electronic, mechanical, photocopy, recording, or otherwise—without prior written permission of the publisher.

Facebook: Ellie St. Clair

Cover by AJF Designs

Do you love historical romance? Receive access to a free ebook, as well as exclusive content such as giveaways, contests, freebies and advance notice of pre-orders through my mailing list!

Sign up here!

Also By Ellie St. Clair

Happily Ever After
The Duke She Wished For
Someday Her Duke Will Come
Once Upon a Duke's Dream
He's a Duke, But I Love Him
Loved by the Viscount
Because the Earl Loved Me

Happily Ever After Box Set Books 1-3
Happily Ever After Box Set Books 4-6

For a full list of all of Ellie's books, please see
www.elliestclair.com/books.

CHAPTER 1

*"When young and thoughtless, Laura said,
No one shall win my heart;
But little dreamt the simple maid,
Of love's delusive art.
At ball or play,
She flirt away,
And ever giddy be;
But always said,
I ne'er will wed,
No one shall govern me.
No, no, no, no, no, no,
No one shall govern me."*

"Interesting choice of song, sister."

Anne let out a yelp as her brother scared the wits out of her. She swirled on the small round stool to the direction of his voice, finding him leaning in the doorframe, arms crossed and a pensive look on his face. She smiled, trying to disarm him, but his raised eyebrow stayed high as he looked at her.

"It's a pretty little tune, Alastair, 'tis all," she said with a shrug, turning back on the stool to the canvas in front of her. She sighed as she looked over the rainbow she had painted. Only, it didn't really look like a rainbow. True, it held all the colors of one, but the landscape in front of her had turned into more of an assortment of splatters, something that was more akin to a child's painting than that of a young woman who was now one-and-twenty.

"And you have a pretty little voice to sing it with, Anne, to be sure," he responded, and she raised her nose in the air at his mocking tone. "Only, if you are not careful, you shall follow in the footsteps of the simple maid of whom you sing and become — how do the song lyrics continue? Oh, that's right — 'a pettish, pert old maid.'"

"Oh, Alastair, do not be ridiculous," Anne said, setting down her brush and giving up on the work. "Olivia was much older than I am now when you married, and that didn't seem to be an issue with you, now did it?"

He snorted in response, and she laughed, for she knew she had him there.

"Not to worry, dear brother, I will marry in time. At the moment, however, my life is far too enjoyable to add a husband to it."

"Have you told Mother this?"

"Of course."

"Mmm-hmm." Alastair didn't look as though he believed her. Nor should he. Anne's older brother knew better than anyone her skill in telling a fib, into making it so believable that nary anyone questioned her. Except him. "You have many young gentlemen who are interested in making a match with you," he continued. "And you told Olivia just the other day that you felt your life was becoming boring, that you were looking for something more."

"Yes," she said slowly, as if he were simple. "And that 'something more' at the moment is not a man." She paused then stood and walked to the sash window, looking out at the lush gardens beyond the glass. They were in the country for the summer season, and she missed the bustle of London, the theatre and the parties, although she did enjoy the leisurely days at her brother's estate. Not only that, but the house parties they had recently attended had included musicales, which she loved to no end.

"Alastair, is there anything in your life that gives you a thrill, a rush like no other? That causes excitement to positively course through your veins?"

He laughed but then stopped abruptly, seeming to realize she was serious.

"Well, yes," he said. "Olivia."

Anne sighed. Her brother just didn't understand.

"For me, that feeling comes not from a man, nor another person, even." She walked toward him now, her arms waving as she tried to make him understand what she was thinking and feeling. "Alastair, I feel that way when I am on stage in front of an audience, whether I am singing or acting. You know how I love the theatre. It is not so much watching others, however, as the desire I have to be on stage *myself*. When I'm in the audience, all I can picture is being in the role, reciting the lines, filling the room with my voice."

He subjected her to a look of incredulity, and she returned his gaze beseechingly, willing him to understand.

"You mean a ... a musicale or some sort of thing, do you not?" he asked, his nose wrinkling as though he feared her response.

"No, Alastair," she said, shaking her head. "I want to be part of the theatre. I want to be in a play such as those we see at Convent Garden. I want to sing and act and entertain people with the skills I have been born with. I want to be an *actress*."

"Anne," he said, his voice somewhat strained as he brought a hand to his head and rubbed his temple. "You cannot be serious."

"I am."

"You are the daughter of a duke, the sister of a duke. You are a lady. Lady Anne Finchley, and you must understand that you will never, ever, be on the stage, do you hear me? And never let anyone else hear what you have said. An actress, Anne? Do you know what kind of women are actresses? Well, I cannot repeat much of it, but they are loose women, women without morals, who typically … have skills beyond the stage. Please, Anne, don't start on another one of your silly notions today."

Anne's heart sank at his words. Her dream was so far beyond a "silly notion," but Alastair would never understand it. He had everything he could ever want. He had an entire dukedom, a wife he loved, a child to come any day now, and he had never had the desire for anything more. But she knew she could never explain that to him.

He sighed, looking at her now with some pity. "You have a beautiful voice, Anne, you know that, and you are very talented on the pianoforte," he said, more gently now. "Those skills are quite useful when it comes to attracting a man and charming house guests and the like. Do not despair — I am sure you will find a husband who would be more than happy to provide you with the opportunity to entertain for the rest of your days."

That was exactly what she was afraid of — that her life would be spent picking out notes on the pianoforte and playing background music at dinner parties. But she couldn't tell him that. No, to get what she wanted she had to convince

Alastair that she agreed with him. It should not be too difficult a feat.

"Very well, brother, perhaps you are right," she said with a pronounced sigh. "As long as I am able to sing, what more could I wish for?"

He smiled tightly, as if he wondered how much truth was in her words but was too scared to question her further due to what she might say. "I am glad you understand. And Anne?"

"Yes?"

"What is that atrocity on the canvas?"

"I call it, *After the Storm*, and I have painted it for you to hang in your office."

He made some kind of strangled sound and practically ran from the room.

* * *

CHRISTOPHER ANDERSON, the Earl of Merryweather, smiled at the staccato clip-clop of the horse's hooves on the path below him. There was something about the sound that was comforting. It was steady, measured, and never missed a beat.

"Atta boy," he said, patting the neck of his horse, Sir Walter. He could always rely on the animal. Christopher had been riding the same mount since his eighteenth birthday when his father had gifted him the horse, only days before his death.

That week had changed Christopher's life forever. He had loved his father — in his own way — but more than that, Christopher had never been one who enjoyed change. As much as he had always known that one day the earldom would be his, he hadn't been prepared to be thrust into the role quite so soon. His father, however, had well prepared him, and it hadn't taken him long to adjust.

All was going according to plan now, he thought, overcome with a sense of joviality as he took in the beautiful English countryside. Autumn was rolling in and with it the changing colors that meant the approach of his return to London. After many seasons enjoying his youth and the company of all manner of young people of the *ton*, he was now ready to follow through on his duty and take a wife. And who would be better than the sister of one of England's most powerful peers, the Duke of Breckenridge?

As his long-time friend, going back to their days together at Eton, Breckenridge had been agreeable to his proposal once he convinced him that he was ready to settle down. He was sure his sister would be pleased, and Christopher could already see her as his lovely bride. She was beautiful, of course, and had all of the connections and dowry a man could ask for. Besides that, she had always seemed amenable, though — if he was honest — a bit dramatic at times. But he was sure that was simply a consequence of her youth.

With the crisp autumn air, a chill had settled in down to his very bones as the sun began to set early in the evening. Christopher could have taken his carriage and been far more comfortable, but he enjoyed the exercise and the fresh air that riding afforded him. Besides, he was in no particular hurry.

He pulled himself from his reverie to look at the path before him. He thought he should be nearing his friend's home by now, as it wasn't particularly far, but he could see nothing in the distance, nor, in fact, any familiar landmarks, though he had visited Breckenridge many times in the past.

"Fletcher!" he called to his valet, who had been lagging behind. Fletcher, not a particularly skilled horseman, pushed his horse to catch up to Christopher, who sighed.

He wasn't quite sure why he kept the valet around. Fletcher was not particularly adept at anything, really, but he was the son of his butler, a man who had proven his loyalty through the years, and Christopher couldn't bring himself to let the son go. He knew it was ridiculous to be so beholden to a servant, but besides his sister, they were really the only people in his life who felt anything like family.

"Fletcher, how close do you suppose we are to Breckenridge's home?" he asked.

"Ah, by my reckoning, My Lord, we passed the turn to Longhaven about three hours ago."

"What did you say, man?" Christopher asked, turning to his valet, horror beginning to fill him.

"I said, we passed the turn to his home about—"

"I heard what you said," Christopher cut him off, bringing a hand to his forehead. "Why, Fletcher, would you not deem it necessary to say anything?"

"Well, My Lord, you seemed to be intent on the path ahead of you, and I didn't want to seem so untoward as to question you."

"My God, Fletcher," he said, shaking his head. "Well, there is nothing to be done now, I suppose, but to turn around. Unless you know of a shorter way from this point?"

"There is a path, 'tis true, My Lord," Fletcher said, his face red from the exertion of trying to stay on his horse for the past four hours. "Although it will be difficult to traverse through the dark. There is an inn less than an hour from here. Perhaps we could stay there through the night?"

"Very well, Fletcher," Christopher said with a sigh, more disgruntled with himself than his valet. It seemed he was forever getting lost, and, unfortunately, he couldn't entirely blame his valet. Nor his footman. Nor any other servant who accompanied him on his travels. No, if there was one thing that hampered Christopher's otherwise orderly life, it was his sense of direction.

Well, one night at an inn wouldn't be the worst event that could happen. He could have been overtaken by highwaymen, or he could have been completely alone and without any companion who had any sense of where they were.

His bride would wait for him one more night.

CHAPTER 2

All was rather quiet when Anne joined her family in the dining room, which was a rare occurrence in the Breckenridge home. After she seated herself next to her mother, Anne lifted her head and looked at them all in turn. Alastair kept lifting his head to peer at his wife with concern, although that was nothing new. Their babe was due to be born very soon according to the physician, a man who claimed himself to be something akin to a midwife. Olivia thought him to be ridiculous, but Alastair insisted that he was reputed to be the best there was. These days, Alastair could think of nothing but Olivia's welfare. Olivia herself was in wonderful spirits, as she always was, thought Anne with affection for the sister-in-law she had loved from the day they'd met.

But at the moment, Olivia was wearing a rather strange expression, particularly when she looked at Anne. It was as if she was inclined to tell her something, yet was unable to do so. She wore a smile, but it seemed somewhat strained, as if she wasn't sure whether Anne would welcome the news.

Anne turned to look at her mother, who was smiling with

a much more satisfied air. Hmmm. Something was not right indeed, and Anne was beginning to be concerned that it had something to do with her. She narrowed her eyes at Olivia. She was her best chance for an ally.

"Olivia," she said sweetly, noting that Olivia was as striking as ever, her rich honey blonde hair piled on her head. "Is there something you wish to tell me?"

Olivia cleared her throat. "There is nothing for me to tell you, Anne. At least nothing that *I* can say." Her eyes flitted over to her husband, and Anne glared at Alastair, who shifted uncomfortably in his seat.

"Out with it, Alastair," she demanded. "Is there something you wish to speak to me about?"

He cleared his throat.

"Anne," he began. "I actually came to see you in the library earlier today to share some news with you, but our conversation went slightly awry."

"Oh?"

"I was going to tell you that you will be attending a house party with Mother in a few days' time."

"I see," she said, though she didn't really. Attending a house party wasn't exactly a particularly exciting piece of news. They received many invitations, and it seemed they were forever attending one party or another. Of course, Olivia and Alastair had not accompanied them lately, but her mother was forever taking her to the homes of acquaintances throughout the countryside.

"And whose house party will we be attending?" she asked of her mother, who gave her a gentle smile.

"We will be going to Aspendale, to Lord and Lady Winterton's."

"That's not far," Anne said without any particular excitement. The Wintertons were dreary, their three daughters overeager and continually throwing themselves at any eligible young man who came within their sight. "Who is to be attending?"

"The usual crowd," her mother replied with a wave, as if it were of no consequence. "Though there is one particular addition that should catch your particular attention."

"And that would be…" Anne asked slowly, her suspicions now on high alert. There was something odd at play here. Her family was a close one and did not normally keep secrets, but Anne sensed they all knew something that she didn't — something that was going to have an effect on her.

"You know my friend, Lord Merryweather?" Alastair asked, and Anne nodded. "I do."

Of course she knew Lord Merryweather. Christopher Anderson had been a friend of Alastair's for what seemed like forever. Their fathers had been acquaintances, and he and Alastair were of the same circles and had attended Eton together. Lord Merryweather was often present at the very same parties and events where Anne found herself. He was charming and pleasant, although not particularly interesting. She had spent as much time with him as she had any other young gentleman.

"Lord Merryweather will be arriving here, first," Alastair continued. "In fact, I expected him hours ago, but knowing Merryweather he has likely become lost along the way. I see no other reason why he would be late, as he is typically most punctual."

"Of course he is," Anne said with a bit of a giggle and an eye roll. Lord Merryweather was as proper a gentleman as she had ever met. He followed every rule of society and frowned upon anything untoward. Which meant, of course, he wouldn't approve of most of her actions, as she liked to make things interesting now and again. She and her friend, Lady Honoria, were forever creating pranks or beginning little rumors to see how far their tales could reach before they were disproven. Sometimes they never were, though Anne was always sure to never besmirch the name of anyone who didn't deserve it.

"So you enjoy the man, then?" Alastair asked with a hopeful look on his face.

"What do you mean, 'enjoy the man'?" she asked, confused now. "He is affable, that is true, but I was simply commenting on the fact that he is as practical, as punctual, as proper as they come. I've never seen a man who follows the rules more closely or who would more strongly disapprove of *me*."

"Actually, Anne, that is not entirely the case," said Alastair, and Anne looked over at Olivia, who was biting her lip and looking at her in unease. "You see, Lord Merryweather will be escorting you and Mother to the Winterton house party, as he has expressed interest in courting you."

"What?" Anne burst out, pushing back from the table and standing so quickly that the flame mahogany chair crashed to the floor. The diamond in the cane inset stared up at her when she looked down at it in surprise. She bent to pick it up, but her skirt caught on the chair's leg and she flailed her arms wildly as a footman rushed forward to assist her. She turned back to the table, hands on her hips as she tried to maintain some bit of respectability so that her brother would take her seriously.

"Alastair," she said, lifting a finger and pointing at him. "You know I have no desire to court anyone right now. We discussed this earlier this afternoon."

"Yes," he said, a pained expression on his face. "But that was after Merryweather had spoken with me and I invited him here. I thought perhaps you would come around once you knew it was he who was interested. Everyone likes Merryweather."

"Why would you not think to discuss this with me before agreeing to his suit?"

"Anne," her mother interjected softly, placing a hand on her elbow. "You have had a few seasons of opportunity to find a husband for yourself. Alastair is simply trying to be of assistance. You are not beholden to Lord Merryweather in any way. Perhaps you could simply open your mind to the possibility of courtship and see what comes of it?"

Anne closed her eyes and her chest rose and fell as she took deep breaths to calm herself, a technique she had found helped when she needed to keep her emotions at bay. She finally opened them to find three sets of eyes upon her; Alastair's looking at her with determination, Olivia's with pity, and her mother's with hope.

"I shall attend the party, and it seems that there is no choice now but to journey there with Lord Merryweather," she finally said. "But I will be honest. While he is pleasant and I'm sure most young women would be happy with him, Lord Merryweather is incredibly boring and far too practical for my liking. I make no promises to encourage him in any way, nor to agree to any suit unless I find him agreeable." She leveled a pointed stare on her brother. "Which I won't."

She sat back down in her now-righted chair with an air of regality to emphasize her point, and sniffed loudly as she looked down at the boiled duck that had just been placed in front of her. She would have liked to have stormed out of the room, but she was quite hungry, and she didn't care to entertain the thought of going without dinner.

The room now silent, she picked up her fork and began eating, ignoring the gazes of her family around her.

* * *

Twenty hours after Christopher had left his own home to begin the four-hour ride, he arrived at Longhaven, the home of the Duke of Breckenridge.

"Here we are, Fletcher," he said to his valet, who wore a look of relief. "We have arrived."

Christopher was surprised to find the Duke himself standing outside the manor doors as he rode up the long drive to the imposing stone estate. Christopher had always been impressed by the perfectly symmetrical architecture of Longhaven Manor, the windows from each wing in alignment, the large Venetian window at the center gazing down upon him.

"Merryweather!" Breckenridge called as he walked down the stairs, and Christopher dismounted to greet his old friend, their arms outstretched as they shook hands. "I was beginning to worry about you."

"Ah, nothing to be concerned about," Christopher said with a wave of his arm. "Fletcher and I simply became a little confused regarding directions is all. But we made it, did we not, Fletcher?" He looked back for his valet, but the man was nowhere to be found, apparently having already ridden off to the servants' entrance, so grateful he was to be finished the journey and off his horse. "It seems I have lost my valet. Ah, well. Jolly good to see you, your grace."

"And you," the Duke said as he led him into the house. "And it's always Breckenridge to you, old friend."

"How does your wife fare?" Christopher asked him, knowing how much the Duchess meant to the man.

"Very well," the Duke responded, "Though I am slightly worried about what is to come, there is nothing for a man to do now, is there? How fares your own estate?"

"Very well," Christopher said with a self-satisfied nod. He took great pride in the upkeep of his home and lands. He had a very capable steward and servants that had attended his family for many years, but he couldn't help from wanting to be involved in all of the day-to-day operations. When he returned he would be sure to receive full accounts from his staff.

"Glad to hear it, Merryweather," Alastair said. "I admire your dedication. I have come around to enjoy this life, but it did take some time, it's true. Whereas you have been a responsible lord for years now. Anyway, come to my office. We have something to discuss. A slight ... obstacle to our plans, I suppose you could say, but I'm sure it's nothing we cannot overcome."

Christopher looked at his friend's expression, which was slightly concerned — an odd look for Breckenridge. They had always been an unlikely pairing, Breckenridge always breaking one rule or another as long as it was in the name of good fun, as he charmed the ladies with his ready smile and sense of merriment. Christopher, on the other hand, would follow along in the amusement but only as long as it broke no rules, had no potential of an ill outcome. Yet, they managed to bring the best out of one another and had remained close through the years.

As Christopher followed Breckenridge into his opulent office, he was slightly discomforted as the rich crimson and gold reminded him somewhat of a woman's boudoir. He took a seat across the large mahogany desk and crossed one leg over the other. He itched to be shown to his room in order to change and settle himself in after his journey, but it seemed Breckenridge was keen to get to the business at hand.

Christopher did gladly accept the glass of brandy Breckenridge poured for him and took a sip of it before stopping himself and setting it back down. Breckenridge raised an eyebrow at him.

"Still not indulging any more than you can handle, Merryweather?" he asked with a laugh. "Some things never change. Now, on to business. I spoke with my sister last evening, and it seems she is ... not altogether agreeable to our plans."

"Not agreeable? What do you mean?" Christopher asked, slightly confused. "Does she not want to attend the house party? That is fine. We can begin the courtship when she arrives for the Season in London after Christmastide. Perhaps—"

"Ah, that is just it," Breckenridge said, interrupting him. "She has not entirely agreed to the courtship itself. In fact, she is rather adamant that she wants to court no one at all, but not to worry. That is simply Anne being Anne. She is rather prone to her ... impulsive ideas, but she'll come around, I'm sure of it."

Christopher raised an eyebrow. Breckenridge seemed to be assuring himself of Anne's acceptance as much as he was him.

"I'd suggest just not pushing it too much on her at the first, hmm?" Breckenridge continued. "Give her some time to get used to the idea. And maybe try not to be so ... rigid."

Christopher stared at him, hardly believing what he was hearing. Lady Anne did not want his court? He had never stopped to consider that she wouldn't. Ladies were always agreeable to him, encouraging his conversation, his flirtations if it came to that. Now, the time was right. Why would she be any different? Before now, he had been too focused on his responsibilities to consider a wife. He had thought that once Breckenridge agreed — and it had taken some time for the man to come around to the idea of his sister being the object of a man's affections — all would be settled.

"But she has always seemed agreeable to me," he said, now thoroughly confused. "Any time we have danced or conversed, she has been lovely, animated, and seemingly enjoying my company."

"This is true," Breckenridge said with a nod. "And I'm sure

she does. Though I will say that she is quite charming with most she encounters."

"And what do you mean, not be so rigid?" Christopher asked, his temper rising slightly now as he considered his friend's words. "I am not *rigid*. I am a gentleman. An earl. I am all that I am expected to be, and nothing more. She should welcome that."

"Yes, but my sister—"

"Is *your* sister, Breckenridge. As long as you agree, what else matters?"

Breckenridge sat back with a tense look on his face. "Well, I'm not going to marry her off without her consent, Merryweather."

"No, of course not without her consent," he said, waving a hand in the air. "I'm not a barbarian. But she should follow your wishes, should she not? She has been out for a time now, what could she be waiting for?"

"Merryweather," Alastair said, his expression softening. "As I'm sure you know, I have been lucky in my marriage. I love my wife more than I could ever have thought possible. I want the same for my sister. And the same for you, if I am to be honest. Would I be pleased if you could find that together? Of course. But you must choose each other. It cannot be forced upon you. Anne has agreed to attend the house party with you. Accompany her. Charm her. And, perhaps, with a bit of good fortune, you will find that you are well suited. Will that be sufficient?"

Christopher sighed. Accompany her and charm her. He supposed it shouldn't be too difficult a task. And if she wasn't agreeable, well then, it was better to know now than once it was too late.

"Very well, Breckenridge," he said finally with some resignation. "Now, where can I find her?"

CHAPTER 3

*L*ord Merryweather hadn't arrived last night.
Strange, thought Anne as she wandered through the garden, stopping to lean over the edge of one of the flower boxes and inhale the dahlias' scent. The late summer, early autumn flowers were now in full bloom and were a beauty of a different sort than those which bloomed earlier in the year. Her brother's gardener was quite adept, and while Anne had no real knowledge of how to grow anything, she certainly had an appreciation for a setting as beautiful as this.

She reached in and picked a dahlia before moving on, choosing flowers at random to create a bouquet she would take to her room.

Anne shook her head as she thought of her hypocritical brother. Alastair had been one of the most well-known charmers of the *ton* only a couple of years ago, before their father had passed on and Alastair had found himself married to Olivia. In fact, it was *because* of his roguish ways that he had gained himself a wife. He certainly hadn't had any desire to settle down until he was forced to. And now he had the audacity to suggest that she be married? And to a man of his choosing?

She sat down on a garden bench, leaning forward with her chin on her fist. If only she could do what she truly desired, she thought with a sigh, and take to the stage. When she saw the women on stage at Convent Garden, she knew that was what she truly wanted to do, what would make her happy in life. To have the opportunity to take on another persona, become someone else entirely — even if it were for but a few hours — what a thrill it would be!

In her youth, Anne had taken part in the odd production put on by children for friends and family, of course, though that was for nothing but play, to while away the time and provide an outlet for their imaginations. Yet it was almost as though she had never grown up — had never *wanted* to leave behind the ideals of childhood. Why did one have to lose that sense of freedom and abandonment simply because one aged? That was what the theatre did — transported the audience back to a time when life was simpler, when love was possible and opportunity awaited.

Of course, now, she was forever being called to the pianoforte, and she did love music and using her voice, but she wanted the opportunity to use her talents for more than entertaining the bored *ton*.

The theatre could be life changing, and she wanted to be part of it. Ever since she had sat in the audience for Sarah Siddon's final performance as Lady Macbeth, she knew what the ache within her was longing for.

But Alastair was right about one thing. The sister of a duke did not become an actress. Despite the fact that many of them were respectable, even married women with families, it was not a profession for a woman of her status. And so she was left wanting.

And now, she would also be warding off the advances of a

determined suitor. Damn Lord Merryweather and his proper, persistent ways. On the bright side, she thought, it wouldn't take much to scare him away, with him being the proper man that he was, and she naturally prone to dramatics.

The more Anne thought of it, the more she realized that, perhaps, this might prove to be quite fun. She smiled at the brilliant sun warming the autumn day and began to absent-mindedly hum a little tune.

NOT WANT TO MARRY HIM? Christopher could hardly believe what Breckenridge had told him. True, he was no duke, but he wasn't far from it. Lady Anne should be well aware of what awaited her in life — marriage to a worthy gentleman. And who could be more worthy than he? Perhaps his friend was playing a prank, Christopher thought, as he strode through the fascinating great room, looking up at the dramatic scenes painted on the ceilings, before continuing down a long corridor and to the magnificent gardens, where apparently Lady Anne was walking. Breckenridge had always been somewhat of a trickster. Yes, that must be it — his old friend was simply playing a joke on him. Once he spoke with Lady Anne and told her of his intentions, she would accept, and all would be well.

Christopher walked through the lush conservatory, pushing through the glass doors to the garden outside, realizing the potential folly of his task. The Duke had a substantial home, of course, and the gardens were fairly large. He could walk through them all day without finding Lady Anne. *If I were a young woman intent on a walk,* he thought, *where would I go?*

Christopher decided to follow the main path, and he

hadn't gone far when something caught his ear. Ah, the lovely sounds of the countryside, he thought, continuing on his way, cocking his head to hear more of the bird's call. The melody floated through the air, enveloping him. How pretty. How — not a bird's call. For a bird did not sing with words. It was more than a melody wrapping around him, urging him down the path and deeper into the greenery. These gardens were like a maze, with their boxes covered in leaves filled with flowers of every color. His own estate had nothing anywhere near so elaborate, but then, he was but an earl, lest he forget.

The song was a siren's call, he mused as he neared, a spell that had captured him in its net. His feet moved of their own accord down the path as the voice became stronger, louder. He turned the corner and came to an abrupt halt.

For there, but some yards away from him, was the lady he had so precisely fit into his plans. Yet in doing so, he had somehow failed to think of her as a woman. He had forgotten how beautiful, how captivating, how alluring Lady Anne was. Dressed in a flowy dress the color of the sky that swirled about her ankles, her sandy-blonde hair was pulled back in an intricate array of braids, allowing a few blonde curls to wisp over her shoulders and around her classically beautiful face. She held in her hand a bouquet of flowers in a medley of colors, their arrangement so unorganized they were almost beautiful in their disorder. She drew next to the small fountain, sitting on the two-foot-high edge of its stone border as she trailed her fingers through the water, her head bent as she looked intently down into the blue glass, as if searching for something, though what, he couldn't be sure.

Christopher had wanted to speak to her, to arrange this courtship properly, but he was transfixed, unwilling to break the scene in front of him that reminded him of a moving painting he would have given anything to have hanging on his walls. He stepped backward to retreat, but as he did so he heard the snap of a twig under his foot, and Lady Anne's head shot up. Her eyes, which he could now see matched the blue of her dress, widened as she took him in. She tried to hastily stand but in doing so tripped on her hem and let out a bit of a shriek as she fell backward and into the fountain behind her.

"For the love of..." Christopher shouted as he got hold of his senses and rushed toward her, where she lay sputtering in the shallow water. Her beautiful dress no longer flowed, but rather was soaked through, molding itself to her body in ways that activated his imagination, though it had long been in disuse. When she lifted herself up, tendrils of hair were now stuck to her forehead, and the bouquet that had been so beautiful in her arms was now stems and petals floating haphazardly through the water.

She looked at him in shock as, before he could think of doing anything otherwise, he stepped into the fountain himself, trying not to shudder as his boots instantly filled with water. He waded over to her, and as he reached down a hand to help her stand, he tripped over his now-heavy boots and came down with a splash. The water wasn't deep — it was but a foot or so — but it was cold and soaked the entirety of his breeches, shirt, and waistcoat.

When he looked up from his position with his bottom on the fountain floor, his elbows behind him as he held himself up out of the water, she was staring at him with her eyes wide and her mouth in a round "O."

"Well," he said, clearing his throat. "I did tell your brother I would fancy a bath."

With that, the corners of her mouth began to turn upward, and after but a moment she let out a long, loud, laugh. It was not the flirtatious, coquettish giggle of most ladies of his acquaintance, but the laugh of a woman who

BECAUSE THE EARL LOVED ME

knew true joy. It was contagious, and before long he found himself joining in.

"It is actually lovely to see you again, Lord Merryweather," she said, and he tried not to balk at the surprise in her tone. "I cannot recall having ever heard you laugh so merrily before."

He sobered at her words, his smile falling. "My apologies, Lady Anne."

"Never apologize for laughing!" she said as she came to her knees.

He hurriedly pushed himself into a sitting position and then stood so he could better help her.

"You have a lovely baritone chuckle, I would say, Lord Merryweather."

He could hardly focus on her words, however, as he was too occupied with staring at her face. Had her eyes always been such a crystal blue, her lips so pink, the bottom one as full as it seemed now? She raised her perfect eyebrows as she looked up at him.

"I should admonish you for startling me so," she said, chewing on that lip that teased him, causing a dull ache to begin growing within him. "However, I realize it was an accident, and if nothing else, you have provided me a great deal of entertainment on an otherwise dull and somewhat despondent morning." She took his outstretched hand and allowed him to help her to her feet.

"I am sorry to hear of anything that troubles you, Lady Anne," he said, holding out an arm to her.

She wrapped her fingers around it as though they were walking to the dance floor of a crowded ballroom and not standing in the middle of a fountain in her brother's gardens.

"Would you like to speak of it?"

"No." Anne shook her head quickly — too quickly, and suddenly it was clear. What was troubling her was his own arrival and interest in courting her. He nearly dropped her arm, but he was too much a gentleman to do so of course, and instead, he led her out of the fountain, helping her lift her sodden skirts over the edge.

"Where is your maid?" he asked her, looking about for something to dry her with, as her lips had turned the slightest shade of blue and she began to tremble slightly from the cold water.

"Inside, I suppose," Anne said dismissively. "I did not know you would be joining me and therefore had no thought to maintain propriety. As I am told, however, it hardly matters anymore, now does it?"

She looked sideways at him with a bit of a gleam in her eye that worried him. If she was not entirely agreeable to this arrangement, then why was she speaking so openly about it?

"Lady Anne, we should discuss—"

"Oh, here is my maid now!" she interrupted, as a girl came running out the door, apparently having been told to find her mistress once Christopher had set out for the gardens. "I must change before I catch a chill, Lord Merryweather. I shall see you at dinner, and then we will set out for Aspendale on the morrow, I believe. Farewell!"

And with that, the nymph was gone, running as fast as she could with the heavy wet fabric weighing her down until she was out of his sight, and Christopher was left with a strange feeling — one that told him his life was never going to be the same again.

CHAPTER 4

*A*nne had to keep herself from racing down the carriage steps and up the drive of Aspendale, home of Lord and Lady Winterton — though not because of the family themselves. They had three daughters, all of marriageable age, and Anne knew the viscount and his wife were desperately trying to marry them off, and they seemed to be having a time of it as the girls were not altogether lovely and actually presented themselves as rather crass.

She knew that she and her mother had likely been invited simply because of their proximity, and the fact that additional females were required to round out the number of men they had invited to partake. It was a bit of a strange time of year for a house party, as the weather had started to turn, but hopefully, it could relieve some of her boredom.

What Anne was truly pleased about was the fact that she would have the opportunity to spend a great deal of time with her friend, Honoria. They hadn't seen each other for months now, as Honoria's family had remained in London. Anne had so much to tell her.

Now, as they entered the drawing room, Anne's eyes lit up as she saw her friend, and she raced over to greet her.

"Anne!" Honoria said as she neared, giving her a warm hug. "Oh, how lovely to see you. It has been an age."

"Don't I know it?" Anne said, pleased that Honoria hadn't changed a bit.

She was as lovely as ever, her glasses sliding down her nose as they always did, and she reached up a long slim finger to push them back.

"There is so much to discuss!" she said in a low voice, pulling Anne to a quiet corner of the drawing room. "I have heard tell that you are being courted — by Lord Merryweather! How could you not have told me? A simple note would have sufficed."

Anne looked around her to ensure there were no ears nearby, but it seemed all were preoccupied with their own greetings. Lord Merryweather himself was speaking with several gentlemen — and of course the Wintertons, who didn't hide their particular interest — and so she turned her attention back to Honoria.

"I didn't know myself until yesterday," she said in a stage whisper. "My brother informed me that Lord Merryweather was coming to escort me here and would begin his suit, and I was completely taken off guard."

"Surely you knew he was interested in you?" Honoria asked, her eyes widening when Anne shook her head. "I knew nothing at all!" she responded. "Though it has been rather ... interesting since he arrived."

"Oh?" asked Honoria, her eyebrow arching. "Do tell."

And so Anne told her of the incident in the fountain, and how altogether humorous it had been.

"I would have hardly thought the man had it in him to laugh at himself," Anne said, a smile coming to her face at the memory. "But laugh he did. Can you imagine, Honoria, Lord

Merryweather sitting in a foot of water, his impeccable attire completely ruined?"

"It would have been something to be seen, I'm sure," a baritone voice sounded from behind her.

At the sight of her own shock mirrored on Honoria's face, Anne whirled around to see the man of whom they spoke, immaculately clad today in a white shirt and gray waistcoat and pants, his warm brown eyes looking out at her from his high-chiseled cheekbones. He was tall, and while not an overly large man, when she had felt the muscles in his arm underneath her fingertips yesterday, they had been hard, strong, and well defined.

"Lord Merryweather!" she exclaimed. "I didn't see you there."

"Of course not," he said, his face stoic, yet Anne thought she could see a slight tug at the corners of his mouth. "Otherwise you would not have been speaking of me, now would you have?"

"I — ah, yes. My apologies," she said, chewing on her lip, unsure of what else to say, though this was what she wanted, was it not? To show him that she was altogether a horrible fit for him? "Have you met my dearest friend, Lady Honoria Smallbrook?"

"I am sure we have met within London circles, but I must have failed to note your loveliness," he said, bringing Honoria's hand to his lips, and Anne gasped at the feeling that stirred in her belly, one that wanted to snatch Honoria's hand away and replace it with her own. That was odd. She wanted nothing to do with this man — so why did she care?

"Lady Anne has been quite welcoming, despite the fact that she was unaware of my impending arrival until recently," he said smoothly. Apparently, he had heard much more of their conversation than Anne had originally thought. "I have been friends with her brother for some time, and I have enjoyed having the opportunity to spend additional time with the family."

As Honoria and Lord Merryweather droned on, Anne's mother, Lady Cecelia, the Dowager Duchess of Breckenridge, beamed at her from across the room, as she tried to subtly point Anne toward Lord Merryweather beside her, as though she were encouraging her to engage him in conversation, to be more welcoming.

Anne shook her head slightly, trying to convey her response that no, she was not interested in Lord Merryweather, and could her mother please leave her be? They made silent signals with one another, an argument so hidden that most wouldn't notice it, but before long Anne realized the conversation in front of her had halted, and both Honoria and Lord Merryweather were looking at her.

"Is everything all right, Lady Anne?" Lord Merryweather asked.

She pasted a smile on her face. "Never better," she said cheerfully. "Now, if you will excuse me, I must discuss something with my mother for but a moment."

She strode off with a swirl of her skirts. She had to do something quickly, or before long she and Lord Merryweather would be as good as married in the eyes of the *ton* and her family.

CHRISTOPHER WATCHED HER GO, unable to tear his eyes away from her beautiful bottom as it swung from side to side while she glided away. The more time he spent with her, the more he was finding her completely breathtaking, which was odd, as she was not entirely the woman he had thought her to be. She was not quite as proper, not quite as polished as he would have expected. And yet.… he looked back at Lady

Honoria, who was staring at him with a smirk on her face, watching him with a knowing look.

"You must be careful to not give her your heart, My Lord," she said to him with a gentle smile. "For as much as I absolutely love her, Anne is most likely to break it."

"I have not given her my heart," he said somewhat indignantly. "I am simply trying to court the woman, although she is making it rather difficult."

"I believe that is her intent," said Honoria with a laugh before she walked away. Sensing a presence beside him, he turned slightly.

"Watson!" he said with some exuberance. "How long has it been, old chap? I didn't know you would be in attendance."

"Would you still have come?" his friend asked in jest, and the two of them laughed as they greeted one another.

"Is something amiss, Merryweather?" Lord Watson asked, and Christopher simply shook his head, bemused.

"Only that I will never understand the complexities of women," he said, and Watson laughed.

"After the Lady Anne, are you?" Watson asked. "That is what the gossips tell me, at any rate."

"I am trying, Watson," Christopher said, accepting a glass of brandy from the servant who appeared beside him and taking a small sip. "But it is proving difficult to find the woman alone and still for more than a moment."

"This evening there is to be a dance," Watson said, a gleam in his eye. "I'm sure if you secure Lady Anne for a waltz, she will have no choice but to listen to you and agree to your courtship. But I must say, Merryweather, I am rather surprised at your choice in a wife. You have never had a desire for anything untoward or unseemly, and Lady Anne has a tendency to be … well, not altogether proper at times. There are many young women here who would more than welcome your suit. The Wintertons have three daughters themselves and are practically throwing them at gentlemen as they walk in the door. I realize Lady Anne is a beauty, but have you not considered another option, perhaps?"

Christopher pondered Watson's words for a moment, he truly did, but found he wasn't ready to give up — not yet, at any rate.

"I made a plan that includes Lady Anne," he said, realizing the stupidity of his words but nonetheless unable to let the thought go. "I shall see to that plan until I determine a change is required."

"Always with your plans and lists, Merryweather," Watson said, shaking his head as he clapped a hand on Christopher's shoulder. "Well, I give you my best wishes. I feel you are going to need them."

* * *

"He's coming," Honoria whispered.

Anne groaned as she looked both right and left to find a path through which to escape.

"And I must say, he looks quite determined," Honoria added as Anne tried to hide behind her.

"Can he see me?"

"Of course, you silly lack-wit!" Honoria said with a laugh. "I'm at least a foot shorter than you, though slightly wider, to be sure. Will you not just speak with him, Anne? If you really do not want to court him, just tell the poor man and he can move on to another."

She should. She really should, and yet the thought of him having interest in another woman brought up that strange sensation once again, the one that had pricked at her when he had kissed Honoria's hand. She sighed.

"I told Mother and Alastair that I would see this house party through," she said. "It's just that he's actually quite a nice gentleman, and I really would prefer not to hurt his feelings."

"If he's so nice, then why are you running away from him?" Honoria asked with some exasperation. "A courtship is not an engagement, Anne. Give the man a chance."

"A courtship may as well be an engagement the way the *ton* look at it, you know that, Honoria," Anne said, exasperated that everyone — even her best friend — wanted her married off. "It is not *him* that I object to. It is the thought of being married. I have other plans."

"Oh?" Honoria raised an eyebrow, "and those would be…?"

"I am going to be an actress!" Anne told her in a conspiratorial whisper. If anyone would understand her motives, it would be Honoria. But to her dismay, Honoria simply laughed.

"An actress? Oh Anne, of course you are an actress — every day!" She must have sensed Anne's seriousness, however, for the laughter died on her lips. "Oh, you mean to actually act? Like on stage? Anne, you are—"

"The daughter of a duke. The sister of a duke. Yes, I have heard it all before," Anne said, rolling her eyes, disappointed that her greatest friend should feel the same as everyone else in her life.

"Well, what are you planning to—"

"Lady Anne."

Lord Merryweather. She had forgotten she was avoiding him. She sighed. Perhaps it was time to go back to her original plan, to convince him that she was not the right woman for him. For it didn't seem she had the heart to simply turn him down.

"There you are, Lord Merryweather. I have been looking everywhere for you!" she said with an exaggerated smile, taking his hands in hers as he stepped back slightly in surprise.

"Ah, yes, well, that's wonderful," he said, though she could sense his hesitation at her sudden exuberance. "I was hoping you would indulge me in a dance?"

"I would love to!" she said, taking his hand and not letting go, which seemed to discomfort him somewhat. "Oh, a waltz! How perfect."

She led him to the dance floor, where only a few other couples were stepping in time to the piano music played by Lady Winterton. Typically, that was where Anne found herself, but she knew the Wintertons were doing all they could to showcase their own daughters and would ensure none would outshine them.

"What a lovely tune, Lady Patricia!" she called out to the girl as they passed by her, and when she turned to look at Lord Merryweather, his cheeks had turned slightly pink from the attention they were attracting. Guilt stabbed into Anne, but she told herself this was much preferred to outright turning him down.

Then he took her in his arms, their bodies as close as could be, and suddenly she wondered if she was making the right decision after all.

CHAPTER 5

What was wrong with this woman? In one moment it seemed as though she was trying to be rid of him, and in the next, she was practically throwing herself at him. Christopher was completely taken off guard, and he did not like surprises. Not one bit.

"Lady Anne," he began, clearing his throat, but stopped suddenly when she pressed herself closer against him, and he looked around them to see if anyone had noticed. It seemed that, at the moment, everyone was intent on something other than the two of them, but he thought that he had better take a step backward. His body, however, betrayed him, as it reveled in his closeness to Lady Anne and her beautiful, sensual curves.

She smiled up a him prettily, and he suddenly forgot what he was going to say as her blue eyes met his, and somehow they actually seemed to twinkle when the flickering light cast from the chandelier overhead reflected off of them.

His step faltered as he held her, turning to her among the other couples in the room that before had seemed fairly large, but now seemed to be closing in as he wanted nothing more than for it to simply be the two of them, here together, alone.

"Yes?" she asked breathily, and he looked down at her, surprised by the sudden change in her tone. Was she mocking him? But no, she certainly *looked* the picture of sincerity. As he recovered his wits, she took the opportunity to fill the silence.

"Did you hear the exciting news? Lady Winterton has arranged an excursion tomorrow night to attend the theatre in Maidstone. I haven't been in forever. Isn't that positively grand?"

Lord Merryweather grimaced slightly. "I cannot say I'm one for the theatre," he said, "though I know many are entertained by it."

Horror covered Anne's face at his words. "You do not like the *theatre*? How can you not like theatre?" He had to smile as she reacted as though he had personally insulted her. "Oh, Lord Merryweather, you are missing out on *so* much life if you do not like the theatre. The intrigue, the drama, the ability to see so intimately into the life of someone else through the skill of an actor or actress — what is there not to like?"

"I cannot say, really," he said with a shrug. "I suppose I'm rather rooted in reality, and it seems silly to waste time on something that has no purpose."

"Well," she said, setting her jaw, "I believe that I must ensure that you overcome your silly notions and learn to enjoy it, to introduce you to the world that art can open up. Tomorrow, Lord Merryweather, I will sit with you and ensure that you come to better understand just how fascinating a play can be. Do you agree?"

"I do. Now—"

"I must say, Lord Merryweather, you are a terrific

dancer," she said, pulling closer to him still, were that possible.

"A terrific dancer?" he said, confused. "I must admit, Lady Anne, that is the first I have received such a compliment. I am a competent dancer, true, but terrific, I am not so sure."

She laughed then, a pretty, merry laugh that drew the attention of others near them, and Christopher cleared his throat a bit nervously.

"Lady Anne—"

"Oh, Lord Merryweather, I must show you something!" she said with sudden glee, and he looked at her with even more bemusement.

"In here?" he asked. "It is a rather opulent great room, I must admit — though nothing like that of Longhaven — but I am not sure what would be here that you would want me to see."

"Not in here, silly," she said, and when he looked down at her, it seemed she was batting her eyelashes at him. Was she flirting with him? Why in heaven's name would the woman resist his attention one moment and then flirt outrageously with him the next? "Come!" she said, once more pulling at his hand, and when he tried to resist, she simply tightened her grip. They were now the center of attention, and he felt the best way to avoid any further gossip was simply to go along with her.

She pulled him into the corridor, and now he did stop, refusing to follow her any further.

"See here, Lady Anne. You must have a care if you do not wish to be the topic of discussion of the entire house party."

"Oh, Lord Merryweather, does it really bother you that much?" she asked, waving a hand. "Follow me, it will be but a moment."

He sighed and did as she asked, walking behind her down

the hallway, growing crosser by the moment. This was not following his plan of courtship. Not in the least.

* * *

ANNE LAUGHED RUEFULLY as she took in Lord Merryweather's face. Why, the poor man was simply beside himself. His brow furrowed as he looked down at her over his elegant, Romanesque nose. Being so close to him, Anne had to admit that he was quite compelling. His dark chestnut hair was cut short, his dress, as always, immaculate. He had chiseled cheekbones and a look about him that none could argue was the definition of a gentleman. She was sorry for him, in truth, but after this blasted party, she knew he would no longer want anything to do with her, as her antics would, of course, not fit with his plans.

The Wintertons had a fine conservatory. Not nearly as extravagant as that of Longhaven, but it included plenty of recessed corners and shadowy nooks that were perfect for what she had in mind.

"Not much farther," she said, throwing what she hoped was a sultry look over her shoulder as she scampered away from him. If she were being honest, she felt a slight thrill of anticipation at the thought of this little rendezvous, though she was nervous at his reaction. If her goal was that he push her away, why did she now feel disappointed at the thought?

She finally found the door she was looking for and slipped through it with Lord Merryweather close behind her. The conservatory was dark, save for the moonlight and the stars that shone through the windows lining the room. Perfect.

"I say, Lady Anne, it is deserted in here. Perhaps we'd best return to the others before we are missed. I wouldn't want to sully your reputation."

"We shan't be long." She began to wander the rows of greenery, searching out something she recognized, some excuse for bringing him here. "Oh, look!" she exclaimed once she found something that served her purpose. "A dahlia. They are my favorite."

"You seem rather fond of flowers," he said, reaching out to stroke a pink petal.

Fire scorched through her as she suddenly envisioned that very same finger upon her skin.

"I-I do?" Her voice came out in a bit of a squeak, and she cleared her throat. *Take on the role of a seductress, Anne, not an innocent.*

"Well, yes. You were collecting flowers in the garden the other day, and now here we are in the conservatory, admiring them once again."

"Yes, of course," she said, attempting to regain her wits as she stepped closer to him. "I do love flowers." She raised her eyes up at him, looking through what she knew were her long lashes. "They are soft, and sweet, and smell so pretty. But in truth, Lord Merryweather, that is not what I wanted to show you."

"No?"

"No."

Summoning all of her courage, she stood on the tips of the toes of her creamy-white slippers, closed her eyes, and brought her lips to his. She had never been kissed before. She supposed she still hadn't, as *she* was the one kissing *him*. He stood still, apparently in shock, and Anne waited for the moment when he would push her away, when he would tell her that she certainly should not be kissing him, that what she was doing was entirely improper and that he wanted nothing more to do with her.

But she had underestimated Lord Merryweather. It seemed that for all his properness, he was not as entirely staid as he made himself out to be. She knew the moment he let his thoughts go and allowed his body to respond instead, as suddenly the stiff, unrelenting gentleman's arms came about her and he took complete control of the encounter. His lips began moving over hers, hard and unrelenting, his hands wandering over her back as he pulled her closer to him. His tongue teased the seam of her lips, and when her lips parted to let out a slight moan, he took the opportunity to ease his tongue inside as if to taste her.

With their mouths tangled in a love play, a sensation unlike anything she had ever felt before began to rise up within Anne. It was as though she suddenly wanted something that she had never known was available to her. She imagined it was like tasting chocolate for the first time — one never yearned for it before, but a little taste only left one desiring even more of it.

As for Lord Merryweather, well, he tasted like peppermint with a hint of the brandy he had been sipping earlier. And he smelled simply divine. If someone had ever asked her how she would describe the scent of a man, she now knew she could say it was like Lord Merryweather — a deep, heady spice such as cloves mingled with leather and musk.

Anne thought she could kiss him forever, and she had an urge to be even closer still to him, as she innately drew against him, pressing herself against the hard edges of his lean body. She paused as something hard pressed into her middle, and her eyes flew open in shock as she realized what it was. Apparently, Lord Merryweather sensed her hesitation, for suddenly his lips broke away from hers.

"Oh, God," he groaned, and gone was the brief interlude, the moment in time when he had lost his sense of reason and allowed freedom to reign. As Anne waited for the words she knew were to come, the realization that she wanted nothing more than to do it all again flooded over her, and she was filled with a sudden sense of despair.

"We should not have done that." There they were, said as his forehead rested against hers, their breath intermingling as they each sought to regain a hold of their reason.

"This was all rather improper." She closed her eyes tightly as she waited for the next bit, the part where he would tell her that this would never happen again, that he was done with her and no longer wished to court her, let alone marry her. She would be free to do as she had originally intended, to chase her dream. She should be welcoming these words. Instead, she now dreaded them.

"Except all I can think of is that fact that I want nothing more than to do it again," he said, and her eyes flew open. "This would be the ideal time to tell you, Anne, that I would very much like to court you, and I am now rather relieved to know that you feel the same."

Well, this was unexpected.

Anne froze at his words, completely unsure of how to reply, as her emotions twisted within her. On the one hand, a sense of elation coursed through her at the knowledge that he wanted her, that he wasn't turned off by her boldness, but accepted it gladly. On the other hand ... this was not what she had envisioned, and all her efforts to scare him away were now for naught. In fact, it seemed she had only encouraged him. She wanted him, true, but did she want to *marry* him?

"I must apologize, Lord Merryweather, I'm not sure what came over me," she said, stepping back from him now, uncertain of what her next course of action should be. "I wasn't thinking. That is something you should know about me. I don't always think things through, you see. In fact, I am rather impulsive. Far too impulsive, many would say. I'm sure you would say so yourself if you got to know me better."

She couldn't help but ramble as he stared at her intently with his light-brown eyes, the color of the chrysanthemums in her gardens. She took a deep breath and decided that the truth, perhaps, would be best. "I am simply saying, Lord Merryweather, that I am really not sure whether we would suit."

He took her hands in his, lifting them to his mouth as he looked down at her.

"I understand your hesitancy, Lady Anne."

Her eyes widened, but she nodded.

"Might I suggest that we simply take the opportunity to better get to know one another and see if, perhaps, there is more between us than it may seem on the surface?"

She swallowed hard, overcome by the intensity of his gaze and the threat of one or both of them becoming very hurt by this arrangement.

"I suppose, Lord Merryweather, that would be fine," she found herself saying.

CHAPTER 6

Despite Christopher's best intentions to spend as much time with Anne as he could for the house party's duration, she proved rather elusive the next day. The woman confounded him. She was right — it certainly didn't seem like they would be well matched to one another. Then she had kissed him. Why, he wasn't sure. From her initial shy, hesitant kiss, so at odds with her personality, she had given herself away. She was not the seductress she was playing at, but a young woman untried in the ways of passion. While he had been taken aback by her forwardness, he was most shocked by his own response to her. He had completely forgotten all reason as his desire for her had taken over. Her words were proving her to be completely wrong for him, and yet he couldn't help but be pulled to her fire, her zest for life that it seemed he had forgotten.

When he was around her, it was as though much of what he thought was so important, that was required to maintain order, no longer mattered quite so much. It was certainly a revelation, and he had an inexplicable urge to share it with her.

If only he could capture the girl alone for a moment.

"You seem rather pensive this evening."

Christopher jumped slightly when he realized Watson was addressing him. They were seated around the dinner table, the air clouded with the smoke of cheroots as the women had retired to the drawing room. Christopher had a glass of port in front of him, though he had sipped it but twice. He had taken things much farther than he should have with Anne last night, and that was with a completely sober countenance. He didn't want to think what he would do were he at all tottered.

"Are you thinking of a particular woman? A lovely blonde beauty, perhaps?"

Christopher knew he probably shouldn't answer Watson, but he decided that if he and Anne would be courting shortly anyway, what did it matter?

"As a matter of fact, I am, Watson," he said, feeling the smile come to his face, and he fought to control it. "It appears things between us may not be as dire as they originally seemed."

"I am glad to hear that, Merryweather," Watson said, a knowing grin coming to his face. "I wish you nothing but the best, you know that."

"I do."

"Well, gentlemen," their host said, rising. "I believe we should make our way to town if we wish to catch the performance."

As much as Christopher was looking forward to spending time with Anne, he really was reluctant to attend the theatre. He didn't understand the draw of watching people onstage make fools of themselves, while the audience worked themselves into a fury of emotion that often led to riots or jeers or other disquieting behavior. He had only ever been to the theatre in London, never in a small village such as Maidstone, and he worried about what was in store. But if this was what made Anne so happy, then he would go and do as he had promised her and attend with an open mind.

* * *

ANNE WAS on the edge of her seat, so excited she seemed to be for the play to begin. It was to be a version of Shakespeare's *A Midsummer's Night Dream*, though what that would be composed of, Christopher wasn't entirely sure. On the carriage ride into Maidstone, one of the Ladies Winterton — they all looked and acted the same, so he wasn't sure which — told him that the theatre company was from London, and were making their way through the country. It gave him hope that they would be, at the very least, fairly competent.

Their party was in a box next to the stage, which seemed a bit crude, but what did he know? Anne seemed to be particularly intrigued by what was to come, as did her friend, Lady Honoria, seated on the other side of her.

Christopher was more interested in the theatre patrons. Every class of person was in attendance, from peers such as themselves in the boxes next to the stage, to the middle class in seats below, to the lowest classes in the pit in the middle. It was a show in itself, he thought, to see the many people all gathered together in one place.

Another Winterton girl was on his other side but she seemed to have given up on him. Apparently, his disappearance last night at the same time as Anne had not gone unnoticed, Watson had told him, and the Wintertons were no longer quite as hopeful in his pursuit of one of their daughters. He was rather pleased about it, for he could hear the lady's shrill voice chattering away with the unfortunate gentleman to her right.

"Cheer up, Lord Merryweather," Anne said, drawing his attention. "This is a comedy. Have you ever seen it before?"

"I have read the play," he responded, "and I cannot say I was particularly fond of it."

He saw her look at Honoria, and he was fairly certain she rolled her eyes, but as the curtains were pulled back, her attention became focused solely on the stage in front of her. Throughout the first act, Christopher hardly watched the play. He couldn't take his eyes off the woman beside him. Her expressions enthralled him. She laughed with undisguised mirth at the comedic parts, shouted along with the crowd when she was angry, and wore her emotions on her face when she was particularly upset about something.

When the curtains closed for intermission, she looked at him with a dreamy gaze.

"Now, Lord Merryweather, how could you not have been entertained?" she asked, and he could respond with all seriousness, "I have never been more captivated in my entire life."

* * *

SHAKESPEARE HAD NEVER DISAPPOINTED ANNE, and tonight was no exception. Even Lord Merryweather seemed to be enjoying himself, she thought, and she hoped she was bringing him around. The theatre company, though not the best she had ever seen, was certainly believable. Lysander delivered his lines to Hermia so lustfully, Hermia herself was lovely and believable, and Anne was enthralled by Puck's antics. She wondered how they remembered the many tangled lines of so many different plays night after night, and wished she could ask the actors themselves.

When Lord Merryweather excused himself for a moment at intermission, she decided to do just that.

Her mother was engaged with some of the other women in an animated discussion, and it was only Honoria who was paying her any attention.

"Honoria," she whispered to her friend. "Follow me!"

"Where?" Honoria asked, but Anne shook her head.

"I will tell you in a moment," she replied. "You shall see!"

Anne led her down the stairs from the box, holding tightly to Honoria's hand as they meandered through the people to the back of the stage.

"Anne, please tell me we are not going where I think we are going," Honoria murmured, and Anne grinned at her friend. "Where do you think that would be?"

"Behind the stage."

"You are right!" Anne said with glee, pleased that Honoria was on board with her idea. Honoria groaned, but Anne knew she would be glad once they had gone through with it. Honoria always said her life would be boring without Anne.

She pushed through the door that led behind the stage, bringing a finger to her lips to keep Honoria silent. Anne wasn't entirely sure what she hoped to gain by this — perhaps just a look into the theatre life, to determine if this was what she truly wanted, or if she was, as her brother thought, simply being fanciful. She wasn't sure if she would actually speak to the actors or not but hoped for a glimpse of them and what it was like behind the stage. She and Honoria tiptoed down the corridor, looking into one empty room before stepping back to continue on their way.

"Are you lost?"

Anne jumped, crashing back into Honoria, but the voice's owner reached out and steadied them. Anne peered at his face through the darkness, finally making him out.

"Lysander!" she said with some astonishment, causing the man to chuckle.

"I suppose, for the next hour or so, I am Lysander to you,

my lady," he said, sweeping out his hand in an exaggerated bow. "I must ask you once again, however, are you lost? The show will resume soon, and I would hate for you to miss a moment of it."

Anne's cheeks warmed, and she was glad it was dark enough that the man couldn't see her well.

"I — ah, that is, we were…"

"You are correct, we are lost," Honoria said finally, and Anne was forever grateful for her much more graceful friend. "It seems we have been turned around. Silly us!"

"Not a problem," Lysander said, and he pointed them back the way they had come. "The stairs are back that way. I shall look for you in the crowd."

"Wait!" Anne said suddenly, needing to know more of this man, of the exhilarating life this man must lead. "Tell me — how did you come to be an actor?"

"I was born into it, really," he said with a shrug. "My mother was an actress, my father a stagehand. It was the life I have always known."

Anne's heart dropped at his words. It was certainly not the life *she* had always known, but how could she find a way into it herself?

"How long are you here for?" she asked, and she saw the surprise in his eyes at her words.

"Only tonight," he said. "Then we will be off for Tonbridge."

"I see," she said, curiosity overcoming all propriety. "Do you think.… could I meet you and some of the other actors after the show? To learn more about what you do?"

"I don't see why not," he said, gracing her with a charming smile that melted any reservations she still held against him. "We will be at the tavern a few hours afterward. Meet us there."

"All right," she said, smiling back, despite Honoria's hiss behind her, "I will."

As Lysander left them, Honoria grabbed Anne's arm with some force.

"You are not actually going to meet him, are you?" she asked, her eyes wide as she turned Anne to face her.

"Of course not," Anne responded, not wanting to worry her friend, but when she turned to face forward, a little smile began playing on her lips as she anticipated the night to come.

* * *

ANNE LIFTED her legs underneath her as the wagon trundled down the broken path, her heart beating wildly in a mix of exhilaration and apprehension. She knew, deep down in her core, that her actions tonight were going to change the rest of her life, though in what way she wasn't entirely certain.

Once they had returned to Aspendale that evening, Anne had feigned a headache and gone to bed, claiming she was tired from the many activities, though nothing could be further from the truth. She had seen Honoria's suspicious look, and she had sensed that Lord Merryweather had turned a bit cold toward her once the play's second half began, but she was too preoccupied to think for long on why that might be. She was determined to finally grasp her life with her own hands and take the chance to explore, for a moment, the possibility of another life, different from that which she had always known, from what had always been expected of her. She had donned a hooded cloak and snuck out of the manor through the servant's entrance, before walking the two miles to Maidstone.

It was foolish, it was risky — and it was exhilarating.

Her Lysander — Lawrence was actually his name, or so he claimed — had been both surprised and seemingly thrilled to see her and had insisted she sit by him while they all partook in a drink. She had been welcomed by the woman she recognized as Hermia — Ella was her name — while Helena, or Kitty, simply stared at her rather frostily. No matter, Anne thought with a shrug, she couldn't please everyone. She had ignored the woman as the others in the company had bought her drinks and answered all of her questions, of which she had so many.

She wanted to know how they all had found the theatre, how they had come together, where they typically performed, and what type of acts they put on. Was it always Shakespeare? No, they said, telling her they did everything from comedies to tragedies to musicals and variety acts.

Anne had been enthralled at that, telling them how much she loved to sing and play the pianoforte, yet she was always reduced to playing only those songs considered proper by her mother, though she didn't share with them that, in fact, it was the *ton* who judged her. She left out the fact she was of a noble family, as somehow she didn't think that would endear herself to the troupe of actors.

"You sing, do you?" Lawrence asked with his charming grin. He really was handsome, Anne thought to herself. When she agreed affirmatively, he stood and held his hand out, insisting she accompany him in a song. She resisted at first, although not too strongly — Anne never turned down an opportunity to showcase her voice.

It was then she knew she had surprised them. As she sang, looking them each in the eye, her lilting soprano joining with Lawrence's silky baritone, she saw faces that had been filled with suspicion and animosity turn to admiration, and it was as though her heart flew as freely as her song.

When Lawrence, who seemed, as far she could tell, to be the group's leader, asked her to join them for their next act in Tonbridge, with the headiness of their admiration, Lawrence's handsome grin, and the alcohol flowing through her blood, she didn't even think as her lips told him yes.

CHAPTER 7

Christopher sat down at the writing desk in his room at Aspendale and picked up his pen. He needed to think, to rearrange his plans. He had thought to court Lady Anne, determine her affection toward him, and then arrange the betrothal.

He sighed. He wasn't so sure anymore. He wanted Lady Anne with a ferocity that he could not deny, but that sort of lust wasn't required for a wife, and there were certainly qualities of far more importance than that — qualities that Lady Anne, it seemed, simply didn't possess.

She was impulsive, impetuous, and her affections, it seemed, changed as quickly as the wind.

Christopher had seen Lady Anne and Lady Honoria begin to head behind the stage, and he had followed them to see what they were up to. He had been close enough to hear her exchange with the actor, had seen the gleam in her eye and had known that she hadn't let go of her ridiculous aspirations to find the stage herself. He had heard her tell Lady Honoria that she wouldn't go to meet up with them. At least she had enough sense to turn down his invitation.

She had watched the play's second half even more intently than the first, her hands gripping the arms of her seat so hard they were nearly white, her eyes fixated on the handsome Lysander as he spouted lines of gibberish. Christopher had barely spoken to her afterward, and she hadn't even noticed.

He picked up his pen.

BRECKENRIDGE,
It is with great regret that I—

THE DOOR OPENED with such suddenness that Christopher jumped in his chair, and he turned around quickly, astonished when he found the recipient of his letter framed in the doorway.

"Breckenridge!" he stood to greet him. "How prosperous. I was just—"

"Have you seen my sister?" Breckenridge barked out, and suddenly Christopher realized just how agitated his friend looked, his cravat completely askew and his blond hair strewn around his shoulders.

"Not since last evening, when we returned from the theatre," Christopher said, worried now. Had something happened to the Duchess? "Has the babe come?"

"No, no, nothing of the sort — at least, not yet," Breckenridge responded, and his mother joined him in the doorway, tears streaming down her face. "It's Anne — she's gone."

"Gone?" Christopher asked, perplexed. "What do you mean, gone? I'm sure she is just—"

"Her bed hasn't been slept in," Lady Cecelia said. "When she didn't come down for breakfast, I thought perhaps she had slept late, but then her maid came to find me, agitated because she had not seen her the entire morning. Oh, Alastair, where could she have gone?"

"Mother summoned me and I came as quickly as I could," Breckenridge said, by way of explanation to Christopher. "I say, man, what occurred last night?"

"A play," Christopher said, confused as to why that would matter. "We went to Maidstone. There was a troupe of actors who came through, performed a bit, and left. They were actually fairly talented, all things considered, though I am not a particular fan of the theatre."

"Good God," Breckenridge said, running a hand through his already thoroughly mussed hair. "That's where she went."

His mouth formed a firm line.

"I'm not sure I understand what you mean," said Christopher, as Alastair pounded his fist on the doorjamb.

"The actors! She went with the actors," he said with a low growl. "She told me some days ago she was going to become an actress, but I brushed off her words, thinking Anne was just being … Anne, with another of her ridiculous notions. She must have seen them and acted on impulse, as she always does."

For a moment, Christopher had no idea what to say, so shocked was he at the idea that she could have even entertained such a thought, let alone acted upon it.

"Do you mean to tell me," he said slowly, "that your sister — the sister of a duke — left this house party with a troupe of actors?"

"Is there something about my words that are difficult for you to understand?" Breckenridge asked, shaking a finger in his face, to which Christopher put his hands in the air.

"I am sorry, Breckenridge, it's just—" he shook his head and placed his hands on his hips, "I just cannot believe it."

"Neither can I," said the Dowager Duchess, her tears now falling in earnest, and Breckenridge ushered her into the room, as untoward as it was for them all to be meeting in Christopher's bedroom.

"I'm sure they can't have been gone long," Christopher reasoned, trying to ignore the pounding in his ears as his heart began to beat rapidly at the thought of Anne, alone, with the dubious characters he had witnessed last night. In an effort to push away his thoughts and emotions, he sat down at the small writing table and pulled out another sheet of paper, beginning to make a timeline of the events.

"We know they began their show at nine o'clock," he said, scratching his pen over the page. "They took a brief intermission and then finished around twelve o'clock. Following that, I heard … oh God. They were going for a drink at the tavern. Anne knew about it and she must have gone. They would have stayed over in Maidstone. Even if they left at first light — somewhat unlikely — to continue their travels, that would have been, oh, say, four hours ago? Right, then, a four-hour head start at the most. But, don't forget Breckenridge, they are traveling with a great many people as well as a cart full of supplies. A man on horseback should catch them fairly quickly. And we know where they are going — to Tonbridge. It isn't far."

He looked up then, to see Breckenridge nodding, though Lady Cecelia was still wringing her hands.

"Thank you, Merryweather, your practicality is actually calming at a time like this," Breckenridge said. "I will leave right away. Good God, Anne could not have picked a worse time to pull a scheme such as this, what with Olivia practically giving birth and—"

"What…" Lady Cecelia interjected, "is it time?"

"I think so," he sighed. "She was complaining of pains when I left. Not that there is anything I can do for her, but I would have liked to have been there just … in case."

Christopher rose, practically ushering Breckenridge out the door.

"Go home to your wife, man," he said. "I will find your sister. I'll take my horse and ride to her quickly. It shouldn't take long."

"You?" Breckenridge turned to him. "I know you are involved in a courtship, but do you really think it is appropriate for you to chase her?"

"We, ah, that is ..."

Breckenridge looked at him expectantly, and he knew that if he were to tell him there was no courtship at all and likely no marriage, the man would never let him go, and would forever hold his sister in contempt if he missed the birth of his child. He hated to lie, but....

"I am sure there will be an announcement of some sort soon," he said, forcing a smile onto his face. "Now go, before you are too late."

A look of relief passed over Breckenridge's face, and he turned to leave, placing a quick kiss on his mother's cheek as he did. "Thank you, Merryweather. Send me a missive as soon as you find her. I will send my carriage after you in order to return her home. Now, all will be fine, Mother." He was out the door and had taken steps down the hall before he reappeared.

"Ah, Merryweather," he said, a look of consternation on his face. "I don't suppose you would consider taking a groom with you? For directional purposes?"

"I'll be fine," Christopher said with a wave of his hand, but when Breckenridge refused to leave, he sighed and finally agreed. "All right, all right, if that should make you feel better, I will be sure to ask for a groom or a footman to accompany me."

"It would," said Breckenridge, and finally he left, back to his wife and soon-to-be mother of his child.

* * *

CHRISTOPHER HADN'T MEANT to lie, but he had difficulty finding a groom who could leave his position without causing too much of a stir, and he knew time was of the utmost importance. Besides that, he wasn't really as bad with directions as everyone made him out to be, now was he?

Or so he had thought. He had heard the actor say they were going to Tonbridge, which was not particularly far away — a couple of hours, at the most. He should have no problem finding them, now should he?

But now he had come to a fork in the road, and he had no idea which way to go. He contemplated one way and then the next, before finally taking a deep breath, sending a prayer up to God, and choosing the left path.

* * *

ANNE ATTEMPTED a smile as she looked into the mirror in the small, dingy room behind the stage of the makeshift theatre of Tonbridge. The actual stage would be outdoors, and they had dressing rooms in the small building behind it, which had been adapted for this particular type of event. She had thought acting would be much more glamorous than this, but so far, it had been nothing but sickness due to the tottering wagon's motion, and the jealousy that came at her from all sides. Lawrence had been more than friendly toward her, and Ella had been the only solace among the company's female members, who, she soon realized, saw her as competition. Everyone else simply glared at her.

She was to sing but one song in tonight's musical, to see how she fared. If all went well, Lawrence told her, they would see whether they might find room for her within their company. Now, through the bright light finding its way through the cracks of the wall's wooden slats, she wondered if this is what she had wanted after all. The life of an actress sounded thrilling, and she did so love performing, but was this the life she was meant to live? Of that, she now wasn't so sure. She sighed, but jumped suddenly when she caught movement in the smoky mirror and realized she wasn't alone.

"Anne, is it?"

Anne turned on the short stool, managing a smile for the tall, blonde woman who stood at the entrance.

"Yes, Kitty, it is."

Kitty sauntered into the room and sat on the sofa across from her, a smirk smearing her face, which Anne thought could have been beautiful if it wasn't fixed now in such a grimace and covered in so much paint.

"Tell me, Anne," she said, her head on her hand, her elbow resting on the table beside her, "what is a girl like you doing in a place like this, with people like us?"

"I am not sure what you mean," Anne said, hearing the nervousness in her voice and attempted to swallow it away.

"I'm an actress, *Anne*," she said, deliberately bating with her name. "I know voices, and I know accents. Your tone is cultured, refined. Your clothing is elegant, of fabric most people will only ever see from afar. You are not of the same class as the rest of us, that's for sure. Did you think you would sneak away for some adventure, is that it? Have a little fun? Or do you really think that you are going to find yourself a place within us?"

Anne laughed nervously, uncertain at what the woman intended by her words.

"I love the stage," she said by way of explanation, "and I would like to see if I have talent."

"I see," Kitty said, leaning forward now. "You do know why you have this solo tonight, do you not?"

"Because Lawrence wishes to see if I perform well in front of a crowd," Anne said, not liking the way the woman looked at her with such hatred blazing in her eyes.

"No," Kitty said, shaking her head back and forth. "It's because Lawrence plans to give you something, but only in order for him to get something back in return."

"I'm not sure what you mean," Anne said, not wanting to admit, even to herself, the likely truth to Kitty's words. She had seen the way he leered at her — so much so, in fact, that she purposely put as much space between the two of them as possible. In fact, in the light of day, she questioned her decision from the night before, but she had already arranged for a note to be sent to Alastair telling him of her plan, and another, more brief, to her mother. She didn't want to admit her mistake. Not until she had her one night on the stage, at least.

"Are you really that stupid?" Kitty asked, raising her painted eyebrows. "Lawrence fancies you, and so you will warm his bed for a time, and while you do, you will get all you want — whichever part, whichever solo, in whichever play you wish. But when he tires of you, well, it will be time for another beautiful young thing to come along and take your place. If you have true talent, you might stick around, as I have, but otherwise, you will be back to the life you left. If you are of rich blood, however, it will never be the same."

"I do not think it's quite like you say," Anne said quietly, angry now that this woman would presume so much about her, without knowing anything of her. She was just jealous. "Lawrence never asked anything of me, and never promised me anything until he heard me sing. I think he truly sees something in me."

Kitty stood, eyebrow cocked.

"Think that if you like," she said, "but I'd watch my back if I were you."

57

And with a flurry of blue skirts, she was gone.

CHAPTER 8

Christopher was sweating through his linen shirt, his waistcoat, and his jacket, despite the somewhat chilled air. The two-hour-long journey to Tonbridge had taken him nearly half a day, so twisted around he had become after he had chosen the wrong path. He sighed as his stomach rumbled painfully in hunger, and he cursed Anne's ridiculous folly. How he had thought he could ever marry such a woman, he wasn't at all sure, but his plans had certainly changed now.

He would not be spending the rest of his life chasing after a woman who thought nothing of running away with not a care for those she had left behind. Her brother and mother were beside themselves. What had she been thinking? He shook his head in disgust.

Christopher now sent his horse trotting into Tonbridge, surprised to find the streets fairly quiet. Was everyone in town at the theatre? He heard the noise of the production before he actually found its source. The open-air structure wasn't as large as the theatre in Maidstone, at least from outside, and it seemed to have been hastily constructed.

Christopher found a boy to see to his horse, and made his way to the opening in the fence, paying for a ticket in the middle seats to enter — he wouldn't be staying long. Just long enough to find Anne and make her see reason.

As he entered, two actors were engaged in a verbal exchange, but the act finished as he pushed his way through the throng of people, and soon a jester took their place. Tonight seemed to be a variety night. He recognized some actors from the previous evening, but he had no time to take a particular interest in any of them or their acts. As he made his way to the stage, he found no entrance to get to the back, and a burly man came over to stand in front of him, crossing his arms.

"Excuse me," Christopher said, mustering all of the authority he could inject into his tone. "I am looking to speak to a woman — one of your actresses."

"As are many men," the man said with a snort, "wait until after the show."

"It's important I speak to her *now*," he said. "She does not belong with the company."

"Sorry, sir, I canno' help you."

Christopher ground his teeth and began making his way back to where he had come from. He would have to go around the back, he supposed, becoming increasingly impatient. He retraced his steps and had almost reached the back of the makeshift theatre when he heard the host welcome a new addition to the show — Annabelle Fredericks. Ann…. His head swiveled to the stage, and he took in a swift breath when he saw her.

She was as beautiful as she always was, even dressed in that hideous costume, a garish green that did nothing for the sandy blonde of her hair that hung loosely down her back, nor what he knew was the blue crystal of her eyes, though he couldn't see them from afar. Despite that, however, she was the most beautiful woman he had ever seen in his life. He cursed his thoughts, for despite all she had done, despite how wrong she was for him, she attracted him more than any other woman he had ever met.

And then she opened her mouth and began to sing.

He was taken back to the day he had come upon her in the gardens at Longhaven, when her voice had called to him, leading him through the lush greenery.

She never turned down an opportunity to play the pianoforte nor entertain a crowd with her voice. But this was different. This was her true voice, the voice of freedom, a voice that spoke to each person in front of her, stirring their souls with her melodies.

And entertain she did. Anne's voice was sweeter than any bird song he had ever heard, her melody beginning slow and soul-stirring, becoming stronger and fuller as she went from one verse to the next. When she hit the crescendo, he realized he was sitting down in a seat, not even sure how he had gotten there, as he was as transfixed as every other man and woman who sat staring. The crowd, which had been lively and vocal through the previous acts, were now silent, captivated by the spell she had cast over the lot of them.

Her song finally finished, and there was just a slight pause before the entire audience broke out into cheers and applause, and Christopher didn't think he had ever seen so radiant a smile on a woman before as Anne's when she graciously accepted their cheers with a curtsy and a slight bow of her head.

When she lifted her face to look at the crowd, her cheeks were bright crimson, and Christopher found himself standing with the rest of the people about him, his hands moving together in movements of their own doing. As Anne lifted her hand in a wave, suddenly a burst of motion from above her attracted his notice, and his eyes wandered away from her to the scaffolding over her head. Time seemed to stand still as he saw the rope begin to swing, at its end a hook that was likely typically used for props or the curtain — he wasn't sure. It didn't matter, as all he could think about was the fact that it was now swinging toward Anne, and she was completely unaware.

Christopher tried to take a step forward, to lift his voice in a shout, to do anything to move her out of the sharp object's path, but it was of no use. He thought, perhaps, at the last moment, her eyes caught his and he waved desperately above her, but was rent utterly helpless as he stood there, staring, with no choice but to watch the horror unfold with his heart in his throat.

* * *

SHE THOUGHT she could see light flickering above her, but when Anne tried to open her eyes, the brightness caused a stabbing pain throughout her skull, and so she kept them closed, tightly, trying instead to sense where she was and what had happened. She breathed deeply as she tried not to panic. In and out, in and out....

It smelled ... moldy, wherever she was, and she could hear only the whisper of skirts and light footsteps hurrying around the room. The more Anne came back to herself, began to recognize what was happening around her, however, the more she began to *feel* as well, and she soon forgot the dull throb of her head as the searing pain on her face settled in, and she squeezed her hands into fists and curled her toes as she continued her deep breaths, trying to keep the pain at bay.

"Anne?" came a gentle voice, one she dimly recognized. "Are you awake? Can you hear me?"

"Yes," she groaned, and she felt cool fingers upon her hand. Suddenly it all came rushing back to her. The freedom of opening herself up to the crowd in front of her, unworried about holding anything back for fear of their judgment, as she always had to when singing among the *beau monde*. The exhilaration of their applause, how much they had loved her. The thrill that coursed through her, finding her true passion fulfilled. Then — had she seen Lord Merryweather in the audience? No, she thought, it couldn't be, and yet a flicker of recognition had struck her as she had looked out, an odd stirring in her heart.

And then all had gone dark. What had happened? Had she collapsed? Had she fainted? She had never been a particularly fragile sort, though she had hardly eaten the previous day as nothing placed in front of her had seemed very appetizing.

"Squeeze my hand if you can hear me." She did. Oh yes, she knew that voice. It was Ella. Anne tried to open her eyes again, and this time it was not quite as painful. Her heart began to beat quickly as, while the light flooded in on her right side, her left eye remained in darkness. Good Lord. Why couldn't she see? Was she—

"There is nothing wrong with your eye, Anne," Ella said, and her cool hand gripped Anne's in reassurance. "I have a poultice on your face, and the cloth is wrapped around your head, covering your left side. As far as I could tell, the eye wasn't affected."

Affected — by what?

"Just — just hold on a moment."

Anne caught a glimpse of Ella leaving her side, and she was able to watch her leave the room, which Anne recognized as the very same in which she had readied herself for her performance. She couldn't turn her head, for then she would disturb whatever it was that was upon her face, but she could hear Ella arguing with someone just outside the door. It wasn't long before Ella returned.

"Anne," she said, crouching beside her. "I don't suppose you know a Lord Merryweather."

So it *was* him she had seen. Anne sighed in resignation and regarded Ella through her one open eye.

"I — I do," she said.

"Do you … want to see him?" She seemed hesitant, which was understandable. Anne had certainly not shared any of her identity with Ella, and she could only guess what the actress must think of her, that a member of the nobility should be here looking for her. Now, whether Anne wanted to see him … that was another question entirely.

"Can you first tell me what happened?" she asked desperately. "Why does my face feel as though it is on fire, and why is there a drum beating on my head? And what have you put over top of me?"

Ella said nothing for a moment, as she brought an arm around Anne's back and helped ease her up into a sitting position on the small sofa. Anne had barely paid it any attention before, and now she truly noticed how torn and dingy it was, and she cringed at the thought of what the stains upon it might be.

"You were singing onstage — do you remember that?"

"I do," Anne confirmed. "I remember all — until after my curtsy, then everything went black."

"There was an accident," Ella said gently. "A rope from the rafters, one that is typically used to haul props up and down, became dislodged somehow and fell. You were standing right in its path. On the end of it was a hook, and it … and you …"

She couldn't seem to find the words but Anne put together the pain that radiated on her cheek with Ella's description of the accident.

"The hook hit me," she said, horror beginning to seep in through her bones as she came to the realization of all that had occurred. "My face, Ella — what happened to my face?"

"You were cut," she said softly. "Deeply, I'm afraid. They brought you back here and sent for a surgeon, but he wanted to bleed you, and I made him leave. My mother, she was a midwife and what they called a white witch in her village. I learned enough from her to know that with wounds, patients often became worse, not better, following a bleeding. I always have some supplies with me — my mother trained me well, though that is a story for another day — and while the season isn't optimal for the herbs I'd prefer, I managed to staunch the bleeding, stitch the edges together, and apply a poultice of yarrow. It should prevent infection and help it heal. I've also given you something for the pain."

Anne listened to Ella's words abstractly, focusing on the situation as though someone else were the patient.

"So it will heal? All will be well?"

Ella paused. "It will heal, in time, but Anne — you will always have a scar. There is nothing that can be done about that."

Anne choked back a cry, at both Ella's news as well as the burning pain that only seemed to be getting worse. She was blessedly distracted, however, when there came a pounding on the door.

"Excuse me, Miss, but I have waited long enough. Unlock this door and let me in *this instant*, or I will be knocking it off of its hinges!"

"Oh dear," Anne said, "I'm not sure I have ever heard the man so upset. You best let him in, Ella."

At Ella's worried expression, Anne tried to smile to reassure her but found it pulled at her face in a rather painful way, and Ella held her hands up in front of her.

"You must keep your face still," she said, her brown eyes

searching the wound as she slightly lifted the cloth to assess the damage. "For the next while at the very least, all right? You mustn't—"

Her words ended in a startled yelp as the door came crashing in behind them.

CHAPTER 9

Christopher flew in behind the door, landing on top of the aged and splintered wood. He let out a groan as he gingerly came to his hands and knees before finally standing, dusting the debris off of his clothes. He hadn't realized the wood was so weak, that the door would give way with the lightest of touches, and his force had propelled him through the opening and into the room. He tried to pull out a long sliver that had cut into his hand and cursed when part of it broke off.

Muttering to himself over the idiocy of his actions and the fact he was even in a situation that would require him to do such a thing, he looked around the dingy room for any signs of life.

He saw the woman first, the one with the long dark, curly hair who had refused him entry, but he didn't care so much about her. He looked past her at the figure lying on the bed, the one who had caused him such consternation.

"Anne!" he exclaimed, forgetting about the pain in his hand and his frustration at being denied entrance to first behind the stage and finally this room. His heart seemed to stop for a moment as she cringed slightly at his shout. She wore the same green dress she had on the stage, only now the bodice was stained with blood, the blood he knew was her own. He couldn't see most of her face, for it was covered in a cloth that seemed to be bound to her head with another long piece of fabric, which looked to be, at the very least, clean.

Since he had seen the rope fall over an hour ago, he had been trying desperately to get to her. He had watched a man from the theatre company pick her up and take her behind the curtain, had seen the actors come and try to revive the show, as he had found his way out of the building and finally found the area for the actors. He had been denied admittance once again, but when he finally began to bellow at them exactly who he was, eventually they began to believe what he said — that he was, as he told them, an earl searching for his betrothed. He had finally been allowed admittance and had looked everywhere for Anne until a tall blonde woman told him with a smirk where he could find her.

And now here she was. She lifted a hand to him in a weak greeting and he rushed over to her, crouching beside her as he ignored the woman sitting on the bed beside her, who had adamantly tried to deny him entrance to this room.

"Anne?" he said, suddenly unsure of how to approach her, of what he should say or do. "Are you all right?"

He cringed mentally at the inane question. Of course she was not all right. He just didn't know what else to ask.

"I'm not sure," she said with hesitation, her visible crystal-blue eye looking out at him. "Ella has done a remarkable job in caring for me, and for that, I shall be forever grateful."

Her voice was flat, monotone, so unlike any words he had ever heard her speak before, for she was normally filled with such enthusiasm and passion for whatever subject it was that she discussed.

"What exactly happened?" he asked, and Anne turned her

head slightly to the other woman — Ella, she had said her name was, and suddenly Christopher recognized her from the play the other night. As Ella softly explained what had occurred, as far as she knew, Christopher realized just how lucky Anne was to be alive. The hook had, apparently, passed by her cheek with enough force to wound her, but fortunately was far enough away to continue its forward momentum. He tried not to think of what could have happened.

And all because he hadn't made it in time.

He looked down at the floor — which he absently noted was horrifically filthy — as the weight of responsibility suddenly lowered itself onto his shoulders. He should have been here hours ago, with more than enough time to take Anne away from this place, before she had even set foot on the stage. Instead, he had been too stubborn, too proud to ask for help, and had been lost for hours. He could hardly look at her for a moment as he thought of it.

"Lord Merryweather?" she asked softly, as he had been silent, sitting beside her in a crouch for more than a few moments now. Part of him felt that he should take her hand, to try to soothe her, while another part wanted to begin pacing the room as he despaired of what he was going to tell her brother. "What are you thinking?"

"Nothing," he said hurriedly. "Simply that I should have gotten here sooner. Your brother put his trust in me."

"Don't be ridiculous," she said, her pert nose wrinkling. "I—"

Her words were cut off as another presence entered the room, and Christopher turned his head to find the actor Anne had so admired, the one who had encouraged this, filling the doorway.

"You!" he said, standing as rage began to take the place of his guilt, and he left Anne's side and began advancing on the man. "This is all your fault. You—"

"Enough," the man said, lifting a hand. A glint caught Christopher's eye as light flashed off a dagger the actor held.

Christopher took a hasty step back. The burly man who had denied him entrance to the stage entered the room and silently stood behind the actor.

"We have to get out of here — now," the actor said, his voice threatening. "The crowd is rioting after Anne's little mishap, and if we don't want to pay for the damage out there and back here, we best be going."

"But Anne can't travel now, especially in the wagon!" Ella exclaimed, to which the actor gave a bark of laughter. "Come now, Ella, you don't seriously believe she is going anywhere with us anymore, do you? Her face is ruined, and no one will pay to see that. I will certainly not be responsible for her care. You, however, we need. Come, Ella."

"We can't leave her!" she said, picking up Anne's hand in her own, and the man glowered at her.

"You either come with us now," he ground out, pointing at the door, "or you will never act again. You will find yourself out on the streets begging for money, or selling your body to the filth that lust after you. I will make sure of it, Ella. You know I can."

She looked as though she was going to say something in response, to stand up for herself, but suddenly the fight went out of her, and Christopher could sense her defeat. At that moment, he felt rather badly for becoming so angry with her earlier, but he reminded himself that she had stood between him and what he had come for. If she had let him into the room they could have been gone long before now, keeping them from further danger.

"Fine, Lawrence, I will be right there," she said and turned back toward them as the man finally stepped out of the room.

"Not to worry," Christopher said, trying to push aside his

own feelings and give the woman some modicum of comfort. What did it matter? They would never see her again after this. "I will be taking Lady Anne home. It is not a far drive, and the carriage is waiting, so she will ride in comfort."

"*Lady* Anne?" Ella asked him, her mouth open, aghast, and when they all turned to look at Anne, she was biting her lip somewhat sheepishly.

"I'm sorry," she said. "I thought that if you knew who I was that you wouldn't be entirely welcoming. I never lied, I just … never shared the entirety of who I was."

"I understand," said Ella with a nod, though Christopher didn't. Why on earth would a woman lie about being of noble blood? It hardly made any sense at all to him. She had what every other woman in England wanted, and yet she would throw it all away for the stage? He shook his head.

"Here," Ella said, picking up a bag in the corner, transferring a strange-looking paste as well as clean cloths into it. She stuffed a gown inside of it before holding it out to Christopher. "The wound must be cleaned and the poultice changed every few hours. Be sure your hands are clean and try to make her eat."

"Thank you, Miss," he said, holding up his palms to halt her efforts, "but I will be returning Anne to her brother, the Duke of Breckenridge, who will ensure that she receives proper care from a physician."

The woman's face fell but she simply nodded, though as she turned to leave, Anne called out to her.

"I will be forever grateful for your help, Ella," she said, "and I will follow your instructions, I promise. Lord Merryweather, take what she offers," she instructed, and when Christopher looked at her, Anne had such a resolute expression on her face that he could do nothing but agree. "And Ella, if there is anything you ever need, do be sure to find me. I live very close, just outside of Maidstone. Ask for my brother, the Duke of Breckenridge, and you shall be led to me."

Ella bobbed her head yes, rushing over to give Anne a long, meaningful, yet gentle hug, before she nodded at Christopher and exited the room, leaving the two of them alone.

"We'd best go," he murmured, to which she nodded, saying nothing as he gathered the few belongings and, despite her protestations, lifted her off the bed. She put her arms loosely around his neck, and after a moment of stiffness, she relaxed into him. As they exited through the back door and rounded the structure, Christopher was relieved to find that the Duke of Breckenridge's carriage awaited them out front of the theatre. It had, in fact, beat him to the theatre, though he had ridden ahead to try to get there faster. When he now helped Anne into it, she sank into the plush cushions, her eye closing as she leaned back. He stepped in and sat across from her.

"I—"

"You—"

They started speaking as one, but when they both abruptly halted their words, a strained silence stretched between them.

"I'm sorry you had to be a party to this," Anne finally said, turning away from him to look out the window. "You shouldn't have come after me."

"I did it for your brother and his wife. Your family members are beside themselves with worry," said Christopher, staring at his fingers, laced together in front of him.

"I sent them a note. My brother should never have asked you to come after me."

"They never received it. And he didn't ask me," Christopher replied, "I volunteered."

"What?" That got her attention, as she turned to look at him.

"It seems his son or daughter was commencing to arrive, and I couldn't allow him to leave his wife."

"Olivia is having the baby?" Anne clapped her hands excitedly, and Christopher was relieved to see a bit of her old spirit revived. "How wonderful," she added softly, wistfully, and he wondered what she was thinking.

"Yes," he said, slightly uncomfortable about discussing such things with her. As it was, now that she was safe, and the two of them were here, together, alone with only the groom atop the carriage as any sort of chaperone, it would be extremely untoward if anyone should happen upon them.

"Lord Merryweather," she said softly, and he looked up to see her gazing steadily at him. "May I call you by your given name? It seems foolish, after all we have been through, for us to continue on so formally. It has occurred to me that I don't even know your name."

"Christopher," he said reluctantly. What did it matter anymore? Proprieties were long forgotten.

"Christopher, then," she said, with just the whisper of a smile on the one side of her lips, and he realized she probably *couldn't* show much expression at the moment. "You said earlier you arrived too late, but you must realize that this escapade was entirely of my own doing, and in no way should you feel any sense of guilt over it."

She was right. This was her own doing, but as she sat there, with her face bandaged and her dress ripped and bloody, he could not very well add to her burdens.

"It's fine," he said, instead, but that didn't seem to satisfy her.

"I mean it, Christopher," she insisted, "I made a poor decision."

A poor decision? That is how she categorized this disastrous ruining of her life?

"I said it's fine," he said, gritting his teeth. "I don't think we should speak of it any longer. I will get you home safe to your brother, and we will deal with any consequences from there."

"If you wish," she murmured. "I must tell you, Christopher, I think — I think one of the actresses did this to me on purpose."

"What do you mean?" he asked, hardly understanding how this woman could continue to converse as if nothing was amiss after suffering such an injury. But Anne's spirit, it seemed, would not be deterred.

"Before the show tonight, Kitty her name is, the tall blonde one, came into my dressing room and was simply awful to me. She said such horrible things. She told me to watch myself." She opened her mouth as if she were going to say more, but suddenly the carriage jolted, and she was thrown across the seat toward him. His arms reached out of their own accord to catch her, and she landed in his lap with an "oomph."

CHAPTER 10

All luck, it seemed, was against them.

After being flung across the carriage, Anne stilled for a moment, taking a breath as she assessed whether or not she had been hurt. She seemed fine, though, as she contemplated the sensations throughout her body, she paid particular attention to Christopher's arms around her. She had to admit that he was being so sweet, concern etched on his face as he asked if she had injured herself any further while he held her, his eyes roving over her.

The groom came to the window to tell them an axle had broken on the carriage, his face turning pink as he looked inside to see the two of them entwined on the seat. Christopher reddened slightly himself, but he made sure she had fully maintained her balance before he helped her down from the carriage, his strong hands grasping her around the waist as he lifted her down and set her on her feet.

Anne straightened her dress as she looked around them, seeing nothing but the English country stretching out around them for miles. It was pretty, she thought, but at the moment, she would have preferred seeing some vestige of civilization as opposed to the open fields. She was tired, she was in pain, and she wanted nothing more than to lie down and fall into a deep, healing sleep.

Not that she would admit any of that to Christopher. She had a fairly good idea what he thought of her little adventure, and she had no interest in adding any further proof to the foolishness of her actions.

She shifted from one foot to the other as she tried to keep standing steadily, but Christopher was more perceptive than she thought.

"Perhaps you should sit back in the carriage," he said to her softly, but she shook her head, not wanting to show any signs of weakness. She had relied on him enough, and she didn't want to leave all of the decisions for the two of them completely in his hands. She heard him mutter something under his breath, so quietly she almost missed it, but he came over to her and placed an arm around her waist in order to keep her upright. She was immediately grateful and didn't realize quite how weak she was until she swayed into his solid weight and allowed herself to relax into him. He smelled divine, she thought, the spicy musk of him filling her senses, and she wondered if she was going to be a bit addled after her accident.

"There is an inn, My Lord, fortunately not far at all behind us. You can't see it from here, but it's just a way around the bend," she heard the groom say. "Night will fall soon, so perhaps you and the lady would like to secure rooms while I see to the carriage? I should have it all fixed by morning."

"Very well," Christopher replied, and then Anne heard him ask the man for directions — very specific directions, she noted.

"Come on, now," he said to her. "Do you think you can

manage a ride? We shall take one of the horses to the inn. It's not far and we'll go slow so you are not jostled."

Anne nodded, so tired now that she was beginning to lose focus. Christopher helped her onto the horse, and as soon as he mounted behind her, she leaned back into him and let herself completely lose consciousness.

* * *

ANNE FELT strong arms come around her, and she smiled dreamily. Was she in a play, in the role of a sleeping princess being saved by her knight in shining armor? Or was this a fantasy of her own doing, a fairy tale come to life? Perhaps she could be a playwright if she was no longer able to act. But why couldn't she act? Wait, something had happened. Her mind began to swim up through the fog, trying to surface into clarity. Something that had forever changed her. But what was it? Suddenly she gasped as she woke, reality crashing back into her. She moaned as pain rushed in and she remembered her accident, the choices she had made, the resulting injury, and Christopher's arrival.

"Steady now," came the voice in her ear, and when she opened her eyes, through her right she could see she was in Christopher's arms, as he carried her through the door of a small, but charming little building. A torch cast light about the entrance and Christopher set her down on a small chair in the corner before telling her to wait for a moment while he secured rooms.

"Good evening," she heard him say. "My wife has suffered an accident and we require lodging for the night."

His wife?

"Have you any rooms?"

"We're a small inn," the man said, "but you're in luck as one opened up but an hour ago. The key for you, My Lord?"

Anne didn't hear anything else, and Christopher's arms came around her once more. The next thing she knew there was softness underneath her back, and she did what she had been craving for hours and fell into a deep sleep.

* * *

Christopher stared down at the woman curled into a ball on the small, but clean bed. Thank goodness they had found a decent, respectable place to stay, despite the fact that their situation was far from it.

He could hardly tell the man she was anything but his wife, for why else would the two of them arrive at a country inn without an escort — not even a maid to accompany them? He hadn't been sure whether he should have asked for one room or two, as nothing could be more improper than sharing a room and yet he knew Anne likely needed someone nearby. The matter had been taken out of his hands entirely when they had but one room available.

She had been sleeping before he had even laid her down on the bed, and he knew that her ordeal had finally caught up with her. Now that they had stopped moving, that he had a moment alone to consider all that had happened, Christopher's emotions roiled within him. His heart had gone out to her today, as they traveled home. He pitied her after all that had happened, had seen how strong she was trying to be despite the pain that had likely overcome her. He had become her protector, a role that he had never seen himself in, though somehow it came completely naturally as he witnessed her suffering. He couldn't, however, ignore the niggling thought at the back of his mind that questioned her actions, wondering just how much he *should* have sympathy for her and how much of this was of her own doing.

Ah well. Now was not the time to concern himself with

any of this. He had already determined that, while he was certainly attracted to her — not only her beauty, but the light she carried around with her wherever she went — she was not a woman who would make an ideal partner for *him*. He would tell her when the time was right. At the moment, he simply had to focus on getting her back to her family without causing any sort of scandal.

Christopher kicked off his boots, took a pillow from the bed, and stretched out on top of his jacket over the small carpet, trying not to think of how many pairs of shoes had likely walked over it before. Finally, he fell into a worried, fitful sleep.

He didn't think he had been out for long when a shriek rent the air, and he bolted up, swiveling around as he tried to determine where danger might lie. He saw nothing, but when he heard a whimper beside him, he turned to the bed, where Anne was rocking back and forth in her sleep, her fists held in front of her with her fingers entwined.

"No, no, make it stop," she murmured, shaking her head back and forth, disturbing the bandage on her face. Her hands came up and began clawing at it. "It hurts … it hurts …. don't let it hurt me anymore. Don't let it fall. Don't—"

"Anne," he said, forgetting all impropriety and practicality as he climbed onto the bed and lifted her onto his lap with the intention of waking her gently as he took her hands in his. "Anne, wake up. You're dreaming. You're all right."

But she wasn't all right. She thrashed back and forth, her hands flying from his as her arms flailed wildly, and he ran a hand over her hair, over her back, as he rocked her to and fro like a child, telling her over and over that she was fine, that he was there, that she should wake. His words seemed to have little effect, however, until she woke suddenly, her visible eye widening in sheer terror, and she clutched at the lapels of his shirt, now open at the collar.

"Oh, God," she cried, tears beginning to leak down her cheek until finally all of the emotion burst out of her in a sob, and she held him even tighter. He did nothing but continue to rock with her, letting her use him, trying to give her all the strength she needed. Finally, her sobs subsided, and she rested her forehead against his chest as he held her tightly.

She sat back from him and looked up into his face, the right corner of her mouth upturned in a rueful, mournful smile.

"I'm sorry," she whispered, "I know that was probably awful for you."

He smiled at her words, for while she was quite correct, he also felt a sense of purpose that he had been able to provide her comfort when she needed it, and he hoped she would be able to overcome her ordeal and find the woman she had always been once more.

"It's fine," he said, seeing the bemused look on her face, and she extricated herself from his grip, sitting back on the bed. "Does your face hurt?"

"Very much," she said, and he noted her white knuckles, the way she gripped the blanket on the bed. "Ella must have applied something to numb the pain, and it has certainly worn off now. What time do you suppose it is?"

He pulled out his pocket watch, walking over to the window to try to make out the time in the faint light of the moon and stars dotting the sky.

"It looks to be shortly past midnight," he said. "Still plenty of time to rest until morning. Your brother's home is but an hour or so away I should think."

"Oh, then we must be at the Best Rose Inn," she said, her hand on her chest as she continued to try to steady herself. "It's not far at all. In fact, I have been before, to the tavern below. Oh, but do not tell my brother that."

"Of course you have," he muttered under his breath, shaking his head.

"What did you say?"

"Nothing," he said, walking over to Ella's bag. "There's a bottle in here, with some sort of potion that your friend told me was for the pain. Why don't you take some, to ease it a bit?"

"I'm not sure," she said, biting her lip. "I want to stay lucid."

"Perhaps it will help you sleep," he suggested, "give you some relief. Lord knows you need it."

She finally nodded, took a swallow, and lay back down. He had just stretched out beside her on the floor when he heard her voice calling his name.

"Christopher? Will you ... will you hold me for a moment?"

He froze. He certainly would not hold her, not in a bed, alone, in an inn in the middle of the countryside. He had comforted her, true, but this would be altogether different.

"Please?"

And somehow, despite all his misgivings, his very nature telling him that this was improper, this was unconventional, this was wrong — he found himself on the bed once more, her body curled into his. If this was wrong, why did it feel so right?

CHAPTER 11

"Did you sleep well?"

Christopher choked out a reply, and Anne wondered about the look of pain that covered his face. "Are you unwell?" she asked, forgetting her own worries for a minute as she looked more closely at him. "You look as though you are going to be sick."

"I'm fine," he said, though he turned away from her as he did up the top buttons of his shirt and pulled on his waistcoat.

She tapped her fingertips on the table, wishing he would give her more than that, but he kept his back to her, rigid and unyielding.

"Christopher?"

"Yes?" he responded, his tone flat, and she hesitated for a moment, but she needed help and her face was itching underneath the bandages.

"I think my wound needs to be cleaned and the bandage changed. Will you do it?" she asked, her words coming out in a rush. She was nervous about what her face might look like, as well as slightly concerned about the fact that she was asking a man such as Lord Christopher Anderson — an earl — to do something so base as to change the bandages on her face, but she didn't know what else to do. She didn't think she could bring herself to do it alone.

"Will you look at it? My face? Ella said it may scar, but I need to know ... how bad it is," she whispered. She had never been one to rely on her looks, but at the same time now that she might always be marred, her heart started hammering in her chest. She knew it was vain to even ask, to worry so about it, but she needed to know.

Christopher turned to her and swallowed hard but nodded, and she sat down on the edge of the bed as he stood in front of her.

"Ella said to clean your hands first," she instructed, to which she saw his lips twitch but he acquiesced, before returning and walking over to her.

He sat down beside her on the bed, his face inches away from her, and her breath hitched at his nearness. How had she slept with him against her all night without feeling a thing? It must have been the draught he had given her. She wondered how he had responded to their sleeping arrangement. He must have — oh. A sudden realization came over her as she remembered his pained look minutes ago. Of course.

Her thoughts on the matter of his closeness fled, however, as he gently began to lift the cloth. Cold air hit her wound, and Anne closed her eyes and sucked in a breath between her teeth as her cheek began to sting and throb once more. When she finally opened them, both of her eyes were uncovered, and she saw Christopher looking down at her, his face flat and unreadable. He dropped his gaze when he noticed her staring at him.

"How bad is it?" she said softly.

"It is difficult to know," he said, hesitating, and for a

moment she wished that he wasn't so honest, that he would lie to her and tell her she looked just fine. "The injury only occurred yesterday, and then there was the stitching, so I'm sure it's inflamed. Only time can heal it now."

"How. Bad. Is. It."

He didn't say anything, but turned from her, gesturing to the smoky, cracked mirror that sat in the corner. She rose, her head beginning to throb all over again as she made her way over to the mirror. When she finally looked at her reflection, she found she couldn't say anything. She couldn't do anything. She didn't gasp, she didn't shriek, she didn't give over to the theatrics she was typically so fond of. Anne simply stood there and stared at the monstrosity that was now her face.

"I'm hideous," she whispered, taking in the long, jagged scar that stretched from high on the left side of her forehead, down beside her eye, to her cheek where it stopped in line with her nose.

"Don't be ridiculous," he said with some force, and she jumped as she turned and faced him.

"How can you say that? Look at me!"

"You are as beautiful as you ever were," he said, some anger behind his tone, which made her pause for a moment before his words sank in. "So you may have a bit of a scar. What does it matter? It's red and raised now, true, but the girl actually did a good job with the stitches, and it will heal in time. As long as you don't do anything foolish to risk infection — and that you allow your brother to send for an actual physician — I'm sure it will be fine. I wouldn't lie to you, Anne. I never do."

She held his gaze, the intensity of his stare, and realized that he truly meant what he said. He was honest to a fault.

"Thank you," she said quietly, "though I must say that I … I understand if you no longer have any wish to marry me."

He paused before he said anything, and her stomach dropped as she sensed his hesitation. His hands came to his hips, and he looked so unlike his usual self with his waistcoat still undone, no jacket, no cravat around his neck. This was how she would see him if she were to marry him. How astonishing to find that the thought no longer caused any anxiety.

Whether she would want to spend the rest of her days as the lady of a house, that she wasn't entirely sure of. But he had been so caring, so kind, so protective over the past day, that, coupled with her surprising, yet growing attraction to him, the thought of him as her husband was not an altogether poor one.

Her stomach knotted, and heat flushed her from head to toe as she waited for his answer.

"Lady Anne," he said, beginning to pace the room. "I do not want to cause you any further distress, but I also do not want to be anything but forthright with you." He stopped and looked at her now. "I do not think, any longer, that we should, in fact, be married — but not for the reason you think. It is not how you look, not at all. I simply do not think we will suit. In fact, I had decided this before I even came to Tonbridge to find you. Our courtship proved to be a failure, as I'm sure you have realized, seeing as you practically ran from me to the stage as soon as one handsome actor said a word to you. That is not the kind of woman I can have for a wife. I need someone reliable, dependable, who will behave like a proper countess. I have a great deal of admiration for you, but I simply do not believe we are a match."

As he spoke, it was as though he was breaking off pieces of her heart one by one, leaving them to fall through her chest, an aching hole left in its place. She stared at him in silence, wanting to flee from the room, but also needing him to realize just how much he was hurting her. But it was not only hurt. A slow burn of anger began to simmer inside her belly as she looked at him, so handsome and yet so … aggravating.

"Look, Anne—"

"Are you actually such a coward?" she ground out, interrupting him. "Just tell the truth and be done with it! You do not want someone who looks like me."

"That is not it at all! As I explained to you—"

"Why did you come after me then? Why did you hold me, comfort me, sleep with me through the night? It was only when you saw the devastation of my face that you decided I was no longer for you."

"That is absolutely not true," he said, maintaining his even tone, which infuriated her all the more. "It was simply the moment when you asked me, which was truly terrible timing I must admit. I wasn't going to say anything until we arrived at your home, but I did not want to lie to you."

She didn't know what to say then, her breath coming in gasps as she willed back the tears that threatened to fall. But she had cried enough in his presence, and she refused to allow any more to come. She tried to breathe much more deeply.

"Anne, I care for you, I do. And if there is ever anything you should need, I will be there for you, I swear it."

She turned from him, stalking to the window and giving him only her back as she surveyed the meadow across the street from them, where the trees rustled in the wind, a few golden leaves beginning to slowly break away from their branches and fall to the ground.

"Here, let me replace your bandage."

"No, thank you."

"Anne, it needs to be—"

"I said, no, thank you."

He said nothing, did nothing, until finally, realizing that

she was being stubborn and that she really did need the stupid bandage replaced, she took her place on the bed once more, set her jaw, and refused to look at him as he went to work, his hands gentle, so at odds with the tension that filled the air between them.

Watching him from the corner of her eye, Anne saw him fumble, and despite her hurt and her anger with him, she did feel some gratitude toward him. This was a task most noblemen would refuse, would feel was too far beneath him. But here he was, proper, ordered Christopher Anderson, Earl of Merryweather, with his shirt sleeves rolled up, crushing paste in a bowl.

It was all so ridiculous that suddenly she wanted to laugh. She had pushed away his suit, and now she found herself pining for the man who had turned her away. In the same breath, she remained, at this moment anyway, completely reliant on him.

"Did you say something?" he asked, lifting his head to look at her, his dark eyes unreadable.

"No."

He nodded and began applying the paste. She flinched a bit, but it actually felt cool when it touched her skin.

"Am I hurting you?"

"No."

"I've sent a note to your brother."

"What?" Her head jerked up painfully at that, her gaze finally meeting his directly.

"I told him that you were well and that we were on our way home. I did not want to worry him. I will leave it up to you to tell him the rest."

"Very well." She swallowed over the thickness in her throat. "What I did … it was awfully stupid. Alastair and my mother must have been so worried."

"They were."

"I wrote notes to them, but Lawrence must not have sent them as he promised. I was caught up in the moment. I didn't think. I just … went."

"I realize that."

She was silent as she contemplated the consequences of her actions. She vowed that whatever happened, she would never again be so reckless, so unconcerned with the feelings of others.

Christopher placed the fresh piece of cloth on her face, wrapping another swath of linen around her head. "There we are. Well, if I ever find myself in need of additional income, it seems I have some nursing skills."

His attempt at levity did nothing to lift her from the sense of melancholy that was beginning to wash over her, the despair at the thought that she was losing all of her options. She could never return to the stage, not now. Christopher no longer wanted her, and neither would any other gentleman — not when they saw her, nor learned of her actions. She supposed all she could do now was be the best aunt she could to Alastair's child, and to live the rest of her days as a spinster. Perhaps she could become a benefactress at a hospital. Or maybe she should become a nun. Yes, that was it. She could—

"Anne."

"Yes?"

"I… I'm sorry this has all happened to you," was all Christopher said as he turned away from her and began replacing all of the supplies back into the bag. "We should go downstairs and break our fast before departing."

"I cannot go down there," she said, her palms feeling clammy. "There will be people there. People who will look at me, who will see my face. Oh, Christopher, what will they think?" Her lip started to tremble and she bit it once more.

Christopher walked over and crouched in front of her.

She supposed she shouldn't call him Christopher anymore. Not when there was no longer any potential for them to be married. But now that she thought of him this way, she could hardly go back to calling him Lord Merryweather once more. Her thoughts were rambling when he took her hands in his, looking up at her.

"Anne," he said in his steady, calming tone, pulling her clenched fists to him so that she was forced to look at him. "Take a breath. That's it. In, out. Now. You've had an accident. Unfortunately, this happens to people, and all you can do now is to deal with it best you can. We will explain it, and others will understand. If you do not wish to tell the full story, when someone asks how it happened, tell them something fell on you from above. It will not be a lie. All right?"

His words broke through her panic, and as she closed her eyes and breathed, she somehow did feel a sense of calm wash over her. When she opened her eyes once more, he was still looking at her, still concerned, and it was then she realized how much she wanted to be with him, how much she needed him in her life. She wanted the very man who she once could have had, who now did not want her in return.

CHAPTER 12

Christopher had never been a particularly emotional person. He prided himself on his stoicism, his ability to look at every circumstance with the sense of calm and sureness required of a gentleman. But when Anne stood and told him she would need his help changing her dress, he nearly let out an expletive that would not be fit for the ears of any lady, even those of Lady Anne Finchley.

It was he that took a deep breath this time as he began to unlace her cheaply made dress. His hands stilled as they brushed the soft, satiny skin of the back of her neck, where tendrils of her hair had escaped the pins that the actress must have hastily pushed into her hair as she dressed the wound.

Despite everything that was so very wrong about her sense of propriety, of her outlook on life, he could not stay away from her. He sighed, his thoughts escaping him as his fingers began to curl into her shoulder, and she jumped at his touch.

"I can manage the rest, thank you," she said, and he suddenly came to his senses at her words, stepping back from her hastily.

"Right, then, of course. If you need me to ... lace you, or button you, or whatever it may be ... just call."

He spun on his heel and walked to the corner, where he stood in agony with his back turned as she finished dressing.

"I'm done," she finally said, and he gave a great prayer of thanks that she only had to change the final layer of her gown and not any of her undergarments. That would have caused him to lose all vestige of control. He began to fasten her buttons, grateful that she couldn't see just how his hands were shaking as he did all he could to rein in his desire. He swallowed as she turned to face him, a shy smile now on her face.

"Well, I suppose that is all I can do for now," she said, her hands clasped in front of her. "I'm ready to face ... people."

He tilted his head and looked at her. He had been honest with her. The scar, now hidden once again, would likely remain, however, he had seen far worse, and nothing could hide her beauty, not once one came to know her and her passion for life. Though he himself had turned away from it, had he not? But that was an altogether different matter.

"Right. Keep up the brave face, lo— Anne."

Good Lord, he had nearly called her love. What was she doing to him? One thing he knew was that he needed to get himself far away from her before he did something he would regret.

* * *

CHRISTOPHER WASN'T ENTIRELY sure what affect his words had on Anne, but he was proud of her in a strange sense as she held her head high and walked into the inn's small dining room where toast, jam, and tea was laid out. The room was fairly empty, save for a few gentlemen passing through and another couple who Christopher guessed to be country folk judging by their attire.

He nodded to them in greeting as he and Anne seated themselves next to them, and the woman wasted no time in leaning over toward them.

"My Lord, my Lady," she said with a nod of her head, an astonished stare on her face as she regarded Anne, who looked back at her with an unease that Christopher had never seen within her countenance before.

"Hello," he said for the both of them, "are you enjoying your stay?"

"Oh yes," the rather buxom woman said, a smile coming to her face as she looked over at the thin man, who seemed quite happy with his recent marriage, judging by the way he couldn't stop grinning at his wife. "We have just been married, you see. My husband's parents were unable to make the journey to see us wed, so we are going to visit them. Take them a piece of cake, as it were. Oh! Would you like a piece yourselves?

"I'm fine," said Anne, managing a half-smile for the woman, "but thank you. And congratulations on your marriage. I hope you shall have a wonderful, happy life together."

Christopher looked at Anne over the edge of his teacup with some surprise. At first, she had shown reservations when the woman began to speak to her, but in the same breath she seemed truly pleased for the couple. He also wasn't sure how she would react to the conversation with them. She had been raised in the family of a duke, but it seemed Anne had no qualms about their class difference. Though, he mused, she had befriended actors without any hesitation, so apparently she judged people by more than their station. He found he admired that about her, and he looked at her with some newfound appreciation.

"Yes," he finally said, as she was looking at him with some question. "Congratulations." He reached over to shake the husband's hand, and the man looked at him with some surprise, but took his grip firmly with his own.

As the wife — Abigail, she said her name was — continued to speak with them, her husband, Fred, tried to shush her, but she told him to leave her be. "They would tell us if they wished us to leave them alone, would you not, My Lord, My Lady?"

Christopher nodded at her as he swallowed his laughter along with his tea. This woman had complete disregard for propriety, but Anne could use a distraction at the moment, and Abigail was proving that Anne's injury made no difference in her desire to speak with her, for which Christopher was grateful.

"My lady, I do not mean to be forward, but I must ask, have you had an accident?"

Until now. Christopher sighed.

"Yes," Anne said softly, "I've injured my face. Scarred it, I'm afraid."

"Oh, you poor thing," Abigail replied, her face filled with pity. "And you being such a beauty, too. Well, you are fortunate to have such a lovely husband to look after you."

"A husband?" Anne repeated, looking at Christopher with some surprise. He gave her an nearly imperceptible nod to encourage her to follow along with his lie. He wondered if she would say anything to him later about his less-than-perfect honesty. She nodded, though Christopher didn't miss the flush that filled her cheeks. "Right, my husband. Yes, he has been ... very helpful."

Anne remained polite but quiet for the rest of the meal, her mind clearly elsewhere. With nowhere else to direct his attention, Christopher spoke at length with the couple, particularly Fred, who was as interested in agriculture as Christopher.

"Do you live near here? I can't say I recognize you," Fred said. "Though you, my Lady…"

Christopher interjected, not wanting news of Anne's visit with her apparent "husband" to spread.

"I have a home not particularly far, but a couple of hours away. Which, I — *we* — should return to shortly. Well, best wishes to the two of you. We should be off."

Christopher rose from the table, helped Anne out of her chair, and held his arm out to her. As they bid farewell to the innkeeper and Christopher gave her a hand into the carriage, he could sense her looking at him.

"Is something the matter?"

"I thought you didn't lie," she said, and when he turned, he saw her right eyebrow quirked.

"I don't — unless it is absolutely necessary. Which, in this case, it was."

"Very well," she said smartly, and Christopher smiled. It seemed she didn't allow much to get by her.

She was silent then, looking down at her hands, interlocked in her lap as her thumbs made circles around one another. He sighed. Whatever was he to do with her now?

* * *

They sat in silence for most of the short carriage ride to Longhaven. Anne figured there was nothing more to be said. She studied Christopher, though he likely didn't realize it. He sat with his gaze out the carriage window, his brown eyes troubled atop his Roman nose, his cheekbones and jawbones, always pronounced, seeming more so today. She had felt the lean muscle underneath his waistcoat and jacket, which were now rumpled due to his lack of valet.

She had entered his well-ordered, planned-out life and completely upended it with her impulsive schemes and rash actions. He had been right. They led to disastrous results, and now because of it, he wanted nothing more to do with her.

Anne leaned her head back against the squabs, the rocking of the carriage lulling her into a calmness that wasn't quite sleep but was relaxing enough to ease her worries ... for a moment at least. As her eyes fluttered closed, she thought she saw Christopher look over at her, but she figured he was simply checking on her wellbeing, gentleman that he was.

When they arrived at their destination but a short time later, Anne was equally relieved and apprehensive about returning to Longhaven. Its copper-colored brick welcomed her like an old friend ready to embrace her, but her heart starting beating rapidly when her brother emerged to stand on the front steps. What would he say? How angry would he be?

She didn't have to wait long to find out, as she had but one foot out the carriage door when he began to descend the stairs, and in a very un-duke-like manner, began running toward her, picking her up when he reached her and squeezing her so hard she nearly lost her breath. "Anne, thank God."

"Alastair! Put me down!" she gasped out.

Finally, he did so, setting her on her feet and placing his hands on her shoulders as he looked closely at her. His blue eyes, so like her own, filled with concern as they swept over her face, stopping on the bandage. "What happened to you? Are you all right? Are you hurt? What—"

"Why do we not talk inside?" she asked quietly, and he looked around at the gathering servants and nodded. He placed a hand on her back, leading her into the house, and as he did so, Anne snuck a look back behind her to see Christopher slowly following behind. Somehow, his presence gave her a sense of calm, of safety, though she couldn't entirely say why. When he lifted his head, however, she averted her gaze, not wanting him to see just how much she longed for him.

CHAPTER 13

The Breckenridge family reminded Christopher a bit of his own, and he wasn't entirely sure how he felt about it. Of course, no one could match Anne's flair for the dramatic, but when he watched her mother practically run down the manor's regal staircase, something strange tugged at his heart as a memory of his youth came rushing back to him.

He was but a boy, perhaps eight years old or so. He had gotten himself into a fair bit of trouble, and rather than face the consequences, he decided he would run away and live in the woods with the foxes and stags, never to return. He had spent about two hours in the damp, gloomy brush of trees by himself before giving up and returning. His mother had been beside herself with worry and greeted him in the same way as the Dowager Duchess currently welcomed Anne.

Funny, he hadn't thought of his mother in quite some time. In fact, he purposely tried not to, for it brought too much pain. She had been gone far too soon, dying in childbirth along with the brother he had longed for. It was that day he had lost his father as well, and his life had never been the same. He was fortunate he had his sister, who had practically raised him.

He smiled as he thought of Ruth, who had always despaired of his lists, of the way he had to have everything just so, but when things fell into their natural order, a sense of satisfaction would fill him, one that he couldn't quite explain to those who didn't understand.

This house, this family — they were just like his own. He hadn't felt the fullness family could bring for some time, and he should leave before he got altogether too comfortable, for this wasn't his life, and the last thing he should do was get used to it.

He donned his hat and turned to leave without attracting any notice, but at that moment Lady Cecelia must have sensed the motion as her eyes alighted on him.

"Oh, Lord Merryweather!" she exclaimed, hastening over to him, much more elegantly now. "We cannot thank you enough for returning Anne to us. How can we ever show you our gratitude? Please, you must stay for dinner this evening."

"I do not think that necessary, Your Grace, but I thank you all the same," he said with a slight bow, not wanting to appear rude. "Tell me, though, how fares the Duchess?"

"Olivia is fine, for now," Breckenridge said, crossing over to Christopher, taking his hand in both of his and shaking it profusely. "She must have been having some kind of strange pain, and we continue to wait. I must say, Merryweather, I agree with my mother. Stay for a bit, will you? I am going to speak with my sister, and then you and I shall have a drink. The butler will show you to your room in the meantime. I arranged for your valet to travel here with your belongings."

Christopher, ever the polite gentleman, could do nothing but nod. As he followed the butler up the grand gilded stairway, he stole a glance down at Anne the very same moment she looked up at him. Her face held such melancholy — it was as though all the light that had shone so brightly within her had been lost in the accident. Christopher didn't realize he had stilled mid-step until he heard the butler in front of him clear his throat ever so discreetly.

"Right," he muttered, "not your concern, anymore, Christopher. Not your concern."

* * *

"Thank you so very much for returning my sister. I shall forever be indebted to you."

Breckenridge handed him a glass of brandy after waving him into the room. Dinner was to be an informal affair, and Christopher had been directed to Breckenridge's office rather than the drawing room.

Christopher shook his head at his friend's words, feeling a thickness in his throat as he wished he could go back and change what happened. He didn't deserve Breckenridge's gratitude. Anne should never have been on that stage — she wouldn't have been, had he only arrived in time. Breckenridge had told him to take a guide, but he had been too proud, too pigheaded, and a very high price had been paid for it.

"Look, Breckenridge, there's something you should—"

"Say no more," Breckenridge said, holding up a hand. "Anne told me about the one room at the inn. I shall compensate you, of course, and I understand why you did what you had to. Anne told me that you were the perfect gentleman, and I must thank you. I knew I could trust you. I promise not a word will escape this family regarding what happened, and your impeccable reputation shall remain intact."

"Thank you," he said, nodding, his frame stiffening. "Though I have no need for any compensation. Breckenridge, in regard to Lady Anne and our previous understanding…"

"Anne told me of your decision," Breckenridge said, walking behind his desk, taking his carved mahogany chair and leaning back in it, one leg crossing over the other. "I understand why you feel as you do, Merryweather. I know you better than nearly anyone. You strive for order, for procedure, and a wife who takes such rash action would not fit into your plans. I only wish…. Well, what is done is done."

"Yes," Christopher said, not sure what else to say. His unreasonable, untrustworthy emotions were begging him to stay, to find Anne and tell her that he would never let her do something so foolish again because he would be by her side to fulfill all that she needed in life. But his mind told him that he should turn and leave this place as quickly as possible before his longing for her became too great. He needed distance, that was all. "If there is anything further that you should need, Breckenridge, please let me know."

He took a step backward as Breckenridge steepled his fingers in front of his face, resting his chin upon them.

"Well, there is one thought…." he clearly caught Christopher's panicked expression as he waved a hand in the air and allowed the front of his chair to meet the floor once more. "Ah, never mind. Pretend I never said anything. Though, Merryweather, I hate to ask you for anything more, but perhaps you would stay a day or two? I could use some help, as I am trying to ensure Olivia is well looked after, while I must also see to Anne's needs. She seemed not herself today, though I imagine it will take some time for her to come to terms with her injury as well as the fact that the life on stage she had naively imagined will never come to be."

Christopher's desperation grew. Nothing good had come out of his association with the Finchleys. They continued to upend and disorder his life in ways that made him panic, and yet how could he turn down his friend's rather reasonable request? He knew some of Anne's despondency was due to his own rejection of her. At the very least, perhaps he could stay for a day or two and help her see the joy that remained in her life, despite all that had changed. Yes, he thought, that would be his new plan. His valet was here, his belongings were here, order was somewhat restored. He would spend two days with his friend's family, and all would be well.

"Fine," he heard himself say and nodded as he continued his backward escape. "Just a day. Two at the most."

"Splendid!" Breckenridge said, clapping his hands together. "Come now, let us join the women."

* * *

ANNE SAT at the pianoforte the next morning, willing the tune to come to her. But it seemed all the light, jaunty melodies she so loved were nowhere to be found. Her fingers began to move of their own accord, and when they did, it was a slow, sorrowful song she played, of tragedy and heartbreak. Last night's dinner had been ridiculous. Her brother had been so disappointed in her. Her mother hadn't said anything besides how happy she was that Anne had returned home, but she continued to reach out to brush a hand lightly along Anne's face. When Anne tried to give her a comforting smile, her mother would simply sigh. Once, a tear even fell from her eye.

The notes Anne played became slower, their minor key wailing. Anne knew her mother loved her, but she also knew that she had always been so proud of her beauty. That was gone now, and her mother was apparently mourning the loss of it as much as she.

And then there was Christopher. Lord Merryweather. The man who refused to leave her alone, despite the fact he had rejected her. It was as though he felt he owed her something after turning her away. But he owed her nothing. He had never promised her anything, and she would never ask for it. Not from him. He had made it clear what he thought of her and she wished he would now just leave her alone.

Her fingers crashed on the keys, in a loud, final chord, and the sharp notes sounded strangely beautiful — so much so, that she did it again, and again. Until, eventually, she realized she was no longer alone.

"If you continue to beat the instrument so, soon you will have nothing to play at all."

His voice, smooth and silky, came from the doorway, and when she stood to face him, Anne schooled her features so as not to betray anything she was feeling.

Christopher strode into the room, his hands clasped behind him. "I seem to recall you were much more skilled on the pianoforte," he said with a slight smile, "or perhaps I was wrong."

Anne shrugged, deliberately keeping her gaze on the gold mantel clock over the fireplace. He was so dapper. He played the role of a perfect gentleman on stage at the theatre. And he was no longer hers, if he ever had been.

"I play what comes to me, when it comes to me," she said. "And at the moment, these are my emotions. I would ask you not to judge them too harshly."

"I am not judging you, Anne," he said with such softness she almost didn't hear him. "I simply miss how you used to play, the joyful girl I came to know."

"She's gone now," Anne said with force as she stood and took a step toward him. "The woman in her place now understands that the world contains harsh truths that are impossible to ignore. That dreams do not always come true. That jealousy and hatred are strong motivators. And that beauty means far more than I once thought it did."

"There is evil in the world, 'tis true," Christopher said slowly, tilting his head as he looked at her, coming another step closer, and they now stood but a few feet apart. "But it needs people like you in it, in order for the goodness to shine forth."

She turned from him, not able to meet his eyes. For there was real emotion shining from their depths, but she thought it was likely only pity. She could take no more of it.

"I thought you would like who I have become," she said. "Less flighty. Less wont to do anything to get what I want. More careful. More proper."

"You cannot change who you are, Anne," he said, "not at your core."

"No?" she raised an eyebrow at him in question. "How do you know this, oh wise Lord Merryweather?"

He smiled at her return to humor, mocking as it was. "Because I have lived it," he said simply. "There have been many times, Anne, when I have not wanted to be the stuffy, boring gentleman that I am. When I have wanted to let go of my inhibitions and simply live, to follow my impulses, take joy where I can. But when I have tried, I am left feeling not at all like myself, and a sense of panic begins to creep in. I find it is better to be the man I am meant to be." He paused for a moment, a look of wonder coming over him. "I have never actually told anyone that before."

She was surprised, and also honored, somehow, that he would share more of himself with her.

"We must do what we can to be happy," she said with a sad smile. "Though sometimes that is out of our control."

Anne saw him open his mouth to respond, but suddenly another voice from the doorway startled her.

"Well, you won't find happiness sitting in here playing music only fit for the dead."

"Olivia!" Anne gasped, rushing toward her. "What are you doing? You should not be up walking around."

Anne's sister-in-law hobbled into the room, her gait as much side-to-side as forward.

"I thought I was going to go mad, lying there in my room for days on end," she said as Anne took her arm. Then she looked at Christopher and nearly began to laugh out loud, as his mouth was wide open in shock at Olivia's entrance in her current condition.

"Then suddenly I realized I was under obligation to no one to remain in there," Olivia continued. "I won't be foolish enough to stray too far, but I may as well find something interesting of which to occupy myself as I wait. Oh, Lord Merryweather, do not be so shocked. You have come to know me well enough to realize that I never do what is expected of me."

Anne did laugh at that, particularly when she saw Christopher swallow his surprise and nod at Olivia.

"Now then," Olivia continued. "I have been staring out my window at the beautiful weather for days. Why do we not sit outside? Perhaps we can have lunch outdoors, what do you think Anne?"

"Oh, I think that would be lovely!" Anne replied, forgetting for a moment about her melancholy. "Shall I ask Alastair to join us?"

"I suppose," said Olivia, "though you must make him promise not to nag at me the entire time. I swear, sometimes, he is worse than a nursemaid."

"He is worried," Anne said. "He loves you so deeply."

"I know," replied Olivia with a gentle smile. "I'm lucky."

A tense silence settled over the room for but a moment until Anne forced a bright smile on her face — as best as she could manage at the moment — and left to find her brother.

CHAPTER 14

"Now tell me, Lord Merryweather, what is your plan?"

The four of them had not wandered far from the house, and Anne had laid out a blanket along with a lunch prepared by the cook. Olivia sat on a chair one of the footmen had brought out for her and was now questioning Christopher.

"Why do you suppose I have a plan?" he asked with a wink, and Olivia laughed.

"Oh, Lord Merryweather, you have always been a charmer."

Christopher, a charmer? Anne wondered at that notion but simply raised an eyebrow at Olivia.

"To be completely honest with you," he said, more serious now, "I am not entirely certain. I believe I will stay here for another couple of days, and then I will return to my estate. I have neglected it for too long, I am afraid. While I have a trustworthy steward, I never feel completely at ease unless I am overseeing things myself."

Anne glanced at him in surprise. Why would he stay? He had no reason to be here any longer. He was not courting her, she was not about to leave, and Olivia would soon be giving birth. It was strange that he would continue on with them, especially with him being a man who so adamantly adhered to all that was expected of him.

"Well, we are happy to have you," Olivia said, and Anne's neck began to ache some from looking up at her.

"Olivia, do you not feel as though you are a queen at the moment, with all of us your loyal handmaidens, sitting at your feet?" she asked, picturing the scene in her mind.

"Are you calling me a handmaiden?" Christopher asked, and when Anne looked at him, he wore a smile.

"You would play the part well, Lord Merryweather," she replied, laughing a bit. "Would you tell us of your estate? I have heard it is lovely."

"Oh?" he asked, "and who have you heard that from? Never tell me, Lady Anne, that all that time I was trying to court you, you were not toying with me, but actually interested?"

Warmth flushed through Anne's cheeks. She hadn't been serious about him at the time, but she *had* been interested to know more of the man who wanted to marry her, that much was true. Not that it mattered anymore.

"I — that is, I—" Anne found herself, for once, suddenly lost for words, and at that moment she heard a groan from Olivia and she jumped up, though she didn't beat Alastair to his wife.

"Olivia, are you all right?" They seemed to speak in unison, and Anne noted Christopher hovering in her periphery, concerned, but still slightly uncomfortable as to how to react to an expectant woman.

"I'm fine," Olivia said, holding up a hand to stem their upset. "Perhaps I have slightly overdone it, that is all. Alastair, darling, would you mind helping me to the house?" She must have noticed Anne beginning to place the food into the basket. "Oh, Anne, you do not need to leave. It's a lovely day, and you should stay to entertain Lord Merryweather. I will be fine, I just need to rest. Alastair will return to you shortly to ensure all is above board, so never fear, Lord Merryweather."

Alastair helped her from the chair, and Olivia waved a hand in farewell. Anne could have sworn that, at the last moment before she turned back toward the house, Olivia sent a wink her way, but it was so quick that she couldn't be entirely sure.

Christopher cleared his throat as he leaned back on an elbow, stretching himself out over the blanket. He actually looked reposed. Anne didn't think she had never seen him reclined before. Well, she supposed he had lain behind her at the inn, but she had been so concerned with herself that she hadn't been paying much attention to him. Shame flooded through her at how selfish she had been, at how much he had done for her, while she barely knew a thing about him. She hadn't bothered to care.

The sun broke through the clouds and struck his face, and she realized just then how handsome he was. She had always known he was good looking, but she had never truly appreciated it until this moment. Her heart seemed to skip a beat, and she swallowed, cursing the bandage that covered part of her face. The physician had visited, and while Anne didn't want any additional treatments, she had been appreciative that he had placed a smaller bandage upon her wound. At the very least, she could fully see now.

And her eyes were full of Christopher, though he was no longer hers to appreciate that way. He had made that clear. She only wished she could erase the memory of his kiss from her mind, for she wanted nothing more at this moment than to feel his lips upon hers once more. She swallowed hard.

"So tell me of your estate, then, Christopher," she

managed, needing to fill the silence, to change her focus. "How far is it? How large is it? Do you have many servants? Many tenants? Does anyone else live there? Do you have many friends nearby?"

Good Lord, now she was rambling like an idiot.

He held up a palm to stem the tide of her questions, though he coupled his response with a smile.

"Very well," he replied. "Gracebourne is not the largest home, particularly in comparison to Longhaven. However, it is beautiful if I do say so myself. The original building dates back to the thirteenth century, and it has been added to throughout the years. Despite its varied architecture, however, the house still seems to flow together. It has been in my father's family for centuries, though I did not spend much time there as in my youth. My mother preferred her own family home, which was much smaller and less grand. She and my grandmother — my father's mother — did not get on well, and my mother abhorred conflict, so we were simply never there. We returned to Gracebourne after my mother passed. But anyway, that is not what you asked about. You wanted to know more about the home."

Anne wanted to tell him no, to continue with what he was telling her, as she was fascinated to learn more about this man and his family. But she sensed that if she pushed, he would close off from her once more, so she let him continue to speak of what he wished.

"Let me see now, what did you ask me?" He put a finger to his lips as he pretended to think hard about what she had said. "Ah yes. First question. It is about a half day's ride from here. If I was to hazard a guess, I would say it is approximately three-quarters the size of this estate of your brother's. I do have a good number of servants, though as it is only me who lives in the house, I do not require nearly as many as other estates. I do have a good number of tenants, and there is a village quite near me, so there are many people around. I have a good number of acquaintances, though most of my friends, as you say, live somewhat farther away. How have I done? Have I adequately answered them all?"

"You have quite the way with lists, Christopher," she said, and when he smiled at her, it was as though he lit a candle within her, so much warmth did she feel.

"I believe that was a compliment," he said, warm surprise coating his words, "for which I thank you."

"I do have one more question," she said, nearly breathless. "Are you ever lonely?"

He paused for a moment.

"All of the time," he said, his voice low and hoarse.

He pushed himself up from the blanket then, coming to his knees in front of her where she sat with her legs bent to the side. She had no control over her actions, as she leaned forward toward him as though there was a rope pulling her in. His hands came up to frame her face, and he ran the pads of thumbs over her cheek. When one brushed the bottom of her bandage, she started, as she had completely forgotten it was there for a moment.

"Oh, Christopher," she said, pulling back slightly and bringing a hand to her face. "I—"

"Shh," he gently ordered, and then hushed any further words by descending his head, his lips covering hers, capturing any further words of refusal.

Oh, Lord, he was wonderful. Today he tasted of chocolate and strawberries, and his spicy clove scent filled her. She was the one who requested entry into his mouth this time, and he opened for her, his arms wrapping around her and she came flush against him. Apparently, he was slightly uncomfortable, for suddenly an arm came around her bottom and lifted her, and she found herself settled on his lap. He tasted, teased, and showed her just how wonderful a kiss could be. Anne had longed for this again, but had never thought it possible, nor had she known that a second kiss could be even better than a first.

One of Anne's arms came around Christopher's back, while the other became entangled in his hair. His dark strands were like silk, she noted as she closed her fist around them. He let out a bit of a groan, and she didn't know where she had hurt him or if it was due to the way their bodies pressed into one another. He was all hard muscle and stiff clothing against her soft muslin dress and sensitive skin.

The play of their tongues could go on forever, Anne thought, and she would be perfectly happy. Then his hand crept between them and ever-so-slightly brushed against one of her breasts, and she nearly jumped up off of his lap. Bolder now and wanting to explore the sensations coursing through her, she took his hand and pressed it against her breast, and while he paused for a moment, likely shocked at her forwardness, it didn't take long for him to overcome any hesitation. He began to lean her backward, down over the blanket, but then the slam of a door in the distance slightly registered in her consciousness. She thought nothing of it, however, until an emptiness replaced where Christopher had been, and she realized he was sitting up, tidying himself, before he reached down and helped her into a sitting position.

"Is everything all right out here?" Anne jumped, so startled she was by Alastair's sudden presence beside them.

"Alastair!" she exclaimed, then realizing she was showing entirely *too* much emotion, she calmed herself and took on the role of a lady — the role she should be playing, she thought wryly. "How — how is Olivia?"

"She's fine," he said, and Anne raised an eyebrow at him. Her suspicions were correct — there had been nothing at all wrong with Olivia. She had wanted to leave the two of them alone together. And apparently, she had known what she was up to, for her ploy had worked.

What Anne wasn't sure of was how she felt about it all. She was certainly attracted to Christopher, and she couldn't deny how much she wanted more of him. As for what a life together would be like ... he had made it clear she wasn't the woman he was looking for, as he didn't want a life of upheaval. Before she attempted to change his mind, however, she should determine whether she could live according to his rules, his propriety, his plans. She tilted her head to study Christopher, who returned her stare with equal intensity. She saw something burning in his eyes, an emotion she felt reflected deeply with her. What would it hurt to see where this could go?

She had forgotten Alastair was standing with them until he cleared his throat, and she turned to look at him. Now was the perfect opportunity to try to make things right.

"Alastair, Chris— Lord Merryweather, I must speak to you of something," she said, holding her head high. She knew it was time to apologize. She didn't like it, and she would do it with dignity, but there was no moving forward until she righted the past. The more she had come to know Christopher, the more she realized *why* he no longer wanted to marry her. She hadn't exactly given him a fair look at what a life together would be like, now had she? She had to prove that she had moved on from the foolish girl she had been.

"I realize that I owe both of you an apology," she said, and she saw the surprise on both of their faces. Was she really that stubborn that they had never imagined they would hear such words from her?

"Pardon me?" Alastair said, his eyebrows rising. "Is my sister, Lady Anne Finchley, apologizing? I don't believe I have ever heard such words from your mouth."

She directed what she hoped was a withering glare his

way before turning to Christopher. It was he she cared the most about. Alastair would forgive her. He always did. At the very least, she had provided him forewarning of her actions, while she had completely caught Christopher unaware.

"I know these past few days haven't exactly gone according to your plans," she said slowly. "I was, at first, absolutely wretched to you, and then you left everything behind to come after me. Thank you for that."

He shrugged, seeming slightly uncomfortable. "Always happy to lend a hand," he said, standing and then doing as he said literally, reaching down to help Anne to her feet. "It's in the past now, Anne. Don't worry any longer."

CHAPTER 15

"I feel as though I am continually being summoned to the headmaster's office," Christopher said as he entered the opulent room, and Breckenridge chuckled from where he stood at the sideboard, glass in one hand, decanter in the other.

"That is all very well, Merryweather, but we both know that you never found yourself in any sort of trouble. I can tell you from experience, however, that the headmaster never poured me a brandy."

"That may be true, but that never stopped you from drinking it in school," Christopher said, shaking his head.

Breckenridge grinned at him with the charm that had always allowed him to extricate himself from his troublemaking ways. He took his well-worn chair behind his desk and motioned Christopher to the seat in front of it.

"I suppose I always had enough to drink for the two of us," he said.

Christopher seated himself, his mirth fading. While he joked with Breckenridge, Christopher couldn't deny that he felt a slight bit of apprehension in meeting with his old friend. Breckenridge wasn't stupid. He would have clearly been aware that something had been occurring between his sister and Christopher. And as Christopher had called off the engagement, what did his friend think of him?

Christopher hardly knew what to make of himself. He had told himself to stay away from Anne, that it wouldn't be good for either of them to give in to their desires. And yet here he remained in her home, sharing laughter and picnics and kisses that nearly led to something more. What had he been thinking? And that, he realized, was the problem. He hadn't been thinking. When he was with Anne, he lost control of his thoughts, his sense of right and wrong, and simply acted according to what he desired at the moment. It left him feeling shaken, although also more … alive than he had ever felt before. It must stop, however. She was injured. She was vulnerable. He was taking advantage.

Part of him wanted to take back the broken-off courtship, to make it whole again. If he did so, there would be no going back. One could not very well break off a courtship more than once with a respectable young lady. Not only would it be abominably frowned upon, but it wouldn't be fair to Anne.

"Breckenridge, I know we planned that I stay for a couple of days, but I feel as though I am now simply intruding," Christopher said, the fingers of his right hand tapping on the desk. "There is no reason for me to be here any longer, and with your wife expecting and a young woman in the house, it isn't altogether proper for me to be here, anyway."

Breckenridge was silent for a moment as he stared at the desktop in front of him.

"What if the young woman was your betrothed?" he asked, lifting his head and challenging Christopher with his gaze.

"We've discussed this," Christopher responded, momentarily stunned, although his heart hammered a bit harder in his chest at the thought of Anne being his. "We are not well suited, and I've already broken off the courtship once."

Breckenridge seemingly ignored him.

"What is the one thing you want, above any other?"

"What do you mean?"

"When you began courting Anne, it was because you felt the time was right to marry, was it not?"

"It was."

"And you chose to break off the courtship because of her accident?"

"Because she proved herself to be a woman who was reckless and impulsive. I don't wish to live a life not knowing what is to come from one day to the next."

Breckenridge sighed, steepling his fingers in front of his face.

"I understand that, Merryweather, I do," he said. "My own marriage was not entirely free of scandal. But life with Olivia has been more than I could have ever asked for. You have been part of the social scene for some time now, always out at a house party or a dance or a dinner. Tell me — do you wish to continue trying to find a woman who will suit you? Why have you not found one yet?"

"I don't know," said Merryweather, sitting back in his chair, his arms crossed over his chest in defense. "The timing wasn't right, I suppose."

"Or the woman, perhaps," said Breckenridge. Then he surprised Christopher by chuckling ruefully. "Ah, Merryweather, for how long did you attempt to persuade me to allow you to court my sister? I denied the idea for so long, and now here I am, trying to push her on you. It's ironic, is it not?"

"I suppose," said Christopher warily.

Breckenridge paused for a moment as if contemplating what he should say next.

"I saw the two of you today — out on the lawn," he said. "I cannot say I was particularly pleased to witness my sister in such a position, but clearly you do have some feeling for her, Merryweather, for I am aware that you are not the type of gentleman to take advantage of just any woman."

Christopher's face warmed and he shifted uncomfortably in his chair, unsure of how to respond.

"I, ah — that is—"

"You could very well have ruined her, Merryweather, if she hadn't been ruined already. There is something I haven't told you — or Anne," Breckenridge said, reaching into his desk drawer and pulling out what looked to be a publication of some sort, and slammed it down on the desk between them. His jovial banter was gone, his smile replaced with the look of a man who had been wronged.

"My sister is destroyed, Merryweather. The scandal sheets have printed all of it," he said bitterly. "I do not know how they learned of her actions, but enough people were present at that house party to know she had gone and that you went after her. Between accounts from servants, actors, and the townsfolk of Tonbridge, it wouldn't have been too difficult to piece together. I was a fool to think this wouldn't come to anything. What gentleman is going to want her now? Think of it. She has spent a night alone with a man, she ran away to the stage, and her beauty is ruined. There is no use in denying it."

He paused for a moment, looking down at his hands, clasped overtop of the offending paper on the desktop.

"I know she did not prove to be the woman you were looking for, Merryweather, but from what I have seen, the two of you seem to be getting on fairly well, and I'm sure you can make a happy life from that. She has behaved poorly, but

BECAUSE THE EARL LOVED ME

she has learned her lesson. You wanted her once. Could you do so again? Your name is now attached to hers, whether you like it or not. I would prefer not to force the two of you onto one another, but rather to encourage you to come together. If you marry her, Merryweather, you will have my sister, which should actually be something to celebrate. For, despite her faults, she will certainly add light to your life. What do you say?"

Christopher said nothing for a moment, as he was stunned into silence. Since he had made up his mind that Anne could not be his wife, he had stubbornly followed along down that particular plan. Breckenridge brought everything back full circle with his words. She had been foolish. She had been impulsive. But had she learned from it? He supposed he had been rather stupid as well, kissing her in full view of the windows of Longhaven. He did enjoy Anne's company, it was true, and he longed for her more than he could describe. Perhaps she had learned her lesson. Perhaps she could be the bride he was looking for.

He contemplated the thought a moment longer, rubbing his chin between his index finger and thumb. He thought of his own house, of the empty halls and silent bedrooms that he longed to fill with children. He had nearly forgotten his mother, and it haunted him that he could no longer remember her voice. The way she used to kiss his wounds, stroke her hand over his hair, and hug him so tightly as a child, however, were memories he would always have. As the thoughts flooded his mind, he could almost picture Anne in the same role with her own children — their children.

"Very well, Breckenridge," he said, extending his hand. "I shall court her once more — if she'll have me."

"Ah, jolly good," his friend said as he shook his hand, relief evident upon his face. "I shall tell Anne the good news."

"Perhaps…" Christopher began, thinking on how Anne

had pushed him away when she had been *told* they were to court, but then seemed to want him more once he had broken everything off. "It may be better to allow me to convince her," he said slowly, seeing Breckenridge raise his eyebrows. "Nothing untoward," Christopher added hastily. "I simply do not think telling Anne will come to any consequence — she must decide for herself that this is the right course of action."

"You're right," Breckenridge sighed. "As I should know. I have been far too concerned about Olivia to look after my sister as I should. Well, I can certainly say I am pleased that you will soon take over that responsibility."

Stricken by the implication of Breckenridge's words, Christopher drew a sharp breath and stared at his friend.

Breckenridge waved a hand. "Jesting, of course. Ah, the fun you will have. Anne enjoys walking to town on occasion. You may have luck asking her to show you around."

Christopher nodded, standing and leaving his friend's office slightly stunned as suddenly the full force of what he had agreed to hit him. Had he made the right decision?

* * *

ANNE TOOK a deep breath as her lady's maid appeared beside her in the mirror.

"Are you ready, my lady?"

"No."

Bridget hesitated at that, but then Anne managed a smile for her and shook her head.

"I only meant that I will never be ready to see myself," she replied. "You can go ahead."

It was time that the bandage come off, time that she see how she looked once more. Ella had told her that once the wound began to close, she should let the air reach it to allow it to heal. Anne took a deep breath as Bridget began to peel back the bandage. It didn't hurt, not any longer, for which she was glad. As to how it now looked....

Anne shut her eyes tightly, recalling the last time she had seen it, hoping that it was much better now. She hadn't been looking in the mirror when the physician had tended to it so she hadn't actually seen it since … at the inn with Christopher. When he told her he no longer wished to marry her.

She exhaled and opened her eyes now, sure she could hear the slow thud of her heart in her chest.

She peered into the mirror. Her scar was no worse, though she didn't think it looked much better. It was still raised, though slightly less red, if anything. Suddenly there was wetness on her face, and she lifted her finger to catch a tear.

"Are you all right, my lady?" her maid asked with concern.

"Yes, Bridget," she replied, determined not to allow her despair to show. "I am simply being foolish. I knew what to expect, and yet I hoped for a different outcome. No matter. Thank you for your help."

Bridget nodded, and after casting a worried look over her shoulder, she left, shutting the door behind her.

What would become of her life now? She supposed she could try again for the stage, only this time she would be playing the role of villains and wicked stepsisters. No one would want to hear her sing, to witness her playing the part of a heroine. She supposed there may be some desperate sod out there still willing to marry her simply for her dowry and the connection to her brother. The moment the thought entered her mind, though, she pushed it away. She would rather spend the rest of her days alone than with someone who cared nothing for her.

Well… she straightened her shoulders. There was nothing else to be done. This was the way of it. With despondence refusing to leave where it had taken root in her core, she stood and left the room, on a mission now to find the housekeeper to tell her to remove the mirror from her chambers.

CHAPTER 16

Christopher felt a strange sense of pride as he looked over at Anne walking beside him. Breckenridge had been right about Anne's enjoyment of visiting town. When Christopher proposed the idea to her, her eyes had lit up with excitement, though it had not taken long for them to dim as she was likely considering that she had not yet been out in a true public fashion since her accident.

When they had walked into the village of Hollingbourne, she had been met by many villagers, curious to know what had happened to her. Christopher felt, however, that this was a much better first outing than within society, scandal notwithstanding. For the villagers had known her since she was a girl and truly seemed to care about her. Anne told them the truth when asked about her scar, and those listening followed along her every word, seeming to feel her sorrow, her anticipation, her glee, and finally her pain.

She still didn't know that her scandal had been found out, and Christopher wasn't entirely sure if and when he should tell her.

There was one thing that he did need to share with her, though he had to be careful not to scare her away.

"Anne," he began, and she turned to look at him. He knew she was upset about her scar, but in actuality, it did nothing to hide her beauty. It simply made her unique. "I know I broke off our courtship at a rather inopportune time. It was wholly insensitive of me, though I did so because I had no wish to continue lying to you." He paused, trying to find the right words. "I have found, however, that I have quite enjoyed spending time with you these past few days, and I thought, perhaps if you are agreeable, may we resume a courtship once more?"

His words sounded stilted and scripted to his own ears, but when Anne turned to him, he didn't miss the look of hope in her eyes.

"Are you sure?" she asked hesitantly. "What about everything you said before — all of the reasons we shouldn't be together?"

He looked down at the ground and scuffed the toe of his boot against the cobblestones. "I made an error."

"Just one?"

He glanced up to see her watching him with her impish grin, the familiar one of old, and relief began to course through him.

"More than one," he replied with what he hoped was a repentant smile, and he realized suddenly how much it mattered to him that she be happy. He still wasn't sure if she would be happy with *him*, or he with her, but his conversation with Breckenridge proved to him that he had to try.

"Sometimes, Anne, I think too much. I am practical, yes, that will never change. But I also need to learn to feel, to let myself find happiness without it being so precisely planned out."

"I don't mind a plan so much, Christopher," she said,

tilting her head and looking up at him. "As long as you realize that plans can sometimes change."

"I suppose if there is a reason for the change."

"Or even if there isn't."

"Yes, well I'm not so sure about that."

They lapsed into a moment of silence until Anne finally broke it with what sounded like a forced laugh.

"Our disagreement on the flexibility of a plan aside, Christopher, I am willing to try, if you are."

"That is all we can do, I suppose."

"You are such a romantic," she said, truly laughing at him.

He chuckled, shaking his head.

"But in truth, that would be lovely," she continued. "Though there is something you must do for me."

"Oh?"

"You must kiss me again."

He stared at her in wonderment.

"Here?"

"No, silly," she said with a laugh, taking his hand and, practically skipping, pulling him off the main street, onto a side path and finally between two buildings. She turned to him, her smile fading into a far more serious look, and while he sensed the rapid rise and fall of her chest, his own breath was now coming just as quickly, and not solely from their rush through the streets. "Here."

She stood on the tips of her toes then, taking his chin in her hands and pressing her lips against his. By God, she was a delicacy unlike any he had ever before tasted. She was willing, she was pliant, she was warm and soft, and everything a woman should be. She fit perfectly in his arms, the scent of rosewater filling him as she kissed him soundly. He had never before encountered a woman who kissed like this. She was certainly not the shy, demure lady that she was supposed to be — and he wouldn't have it any other way.

There was surely one reason to marry her — he wanted her with a desperation he could hardly describe. The thought that she could be his, that he could have her at any time, nearly made him take her right there on the village street. Good Lord, what was she doing to him, this woman who made him lose all of his inhibitions, all of his sense and reason?

But he couldn't stop. He plundered her mouth with his tongue, taking the control away from her. He took her hands in his, interlocking their fingers as he raised her arms and held them over her head, pushing her back against the stone wall. He felt her soft body beneath him, and he groaned as she moved against him.

If he went any farther, he would take her right here and now, and with his last vestige of control, he broke away from her, bringing his forehead to rest against hers.

"You are a siren," he whispered, breathing heavily, "what have you done to me?"

She laughed softly. "I think I like courting, Christopher," she said, and he could feel her smile against his lips. "I never thought it could be like this."

"It shouldn't be," he said, shaking his head. "But somehow with you, nothing is as it should be."

And that was the crux of the matter.

Suddenly a whistle pierced through the air, shattering the magic of the moment, and Christopher jumped back, away from her. He turned his head to see a group of boys gathered at the entrance to the small break between buildings, and when they caught him looking at them, they began to giggle.

"Off with you!" he shouted, though with more laughter than anger, and they scurried away, the echoes of their mirth trailing behind them.

When Christopher turned back to Anne, she was laughing herself, and he sighed with some chagrin.

"We've been found out, it seems," he said, offering his arm to her. "Shall we continue our walk, my lady, or are you going to tempt me into something even more scandalous?"

"We shall continue on," she said, tilting her head to the side and looping her arm through his. "I promise to be good."

His world had been completely turned around. But somehow, for once, it didn't seem to matter.

* * *

She should never have dissuaded Christopher from courting her the first time, Anne thought as they walked through the street, smiling and nodding at villagers along the way. His kisses were heavenly. She would never have imagined that a man such as him, so proper and restrained, could kiss with such abandon. As she looked up at him, his beautiful, defined features made softer by the slight smile he now wore on his lips, she knew she wanted more. And damn it all, if that's what she wanted, she would make it happen.

"Oh, Christopher, what do you think is happening there?" she asked, and he looked as confused as she at the people gathered around the general store's entrance. She pulled him closer, squirming through the crowd. Her eyes widened as she read the poster that had been affixed to the side window.

The words finally registering, she took a step back. Then another. And another. Until finally, just when her eyes closed and she thought she was likely going to fall over in a faint, strong hands caught her.

"Anne? Anne, what is it? Are you all right?"

She opened her eyes to see Christopher peering down at her. She managed a slight nod, and he lifted her and helped her away from the crowd to sit on the building's steps.

Anne took a deep breath in an attempt to compose herself.

"They're coming back."

"Who is coming back?"

"The actors. Lawrence. Ella. *Kitty*. All of them." She felt the panic in her chest at the thought of seeing them again, of the woman who had nearly killed her, and all over a stupid bit of jealousy.

"Are you sure it's them?"

"I'm sure. The name of their company was affixed to it. They're not coming here, but to Chatham, which isn't far. They must have looped around in their travels. I cannot see them again, Christopher, I simply can't."

"It's all right," he said reassuringly, and suddenly she noted the pressure from his firm grip on her hand. "There is no reason you need to encounter any of them. You simply will stay far from the town. They do not even know you live here, remember — when we saw them, we were in Tonbridge."

"I suppose you are right," she said, thinking on it. Only Ella knew her true identity, and she wouldn't tell the rest of them, would she? The panic in her breast began to ease, although as it did, it was being replaced by something else, and while she didn't want to see them again, there was something she needed.

"Although I would like to see Ella again, to thank her," she said slowly. "And there's something else. Christopher ... I need to find a resolution. I want to face her again — Kitty. To make her admit to me what she did."

His face hardened slightly at her words.

"I'm not sure about that, Anne. Think of what the woman did to you. She's dangerous. You would be far better off to put her in the past, to never see her again."

Of course, he would say that. The man avoided confrontation, avoided anything that upset the perfectly planned life he led.

"You don't understand," she said, standing, no longer feeling faint as the anger toward Kitty rushed in, taking its place. "She ruined everything for me. My face, my dreams, any opportunity I had to fulfill my lifelong wish. At the very least, I must make her admit her wrongdoing."

He stood facing her, his eyes narrowed and his lips drawn in a thin, firm line. At first, she thought he was angry, but then she realized he was actually hurt.

"Your dreams? Your lifelong wish? Is that still what you want, Anne?" he asked. "You agree to court me now, when what you really want has been taken away from you, is that it?"

A heavy weight descended on her heart as she thought about what she had said, how it had sounded. "That's not what I meant," she said, reaching a hand out toward him. "It was my dream, but no longer. And that doesn't mean that being with you and being on stage have to be separate paths in life. Whether or not I will ever act or sing again, I still want to be with you, Christopher, surely you must realize that. Before, I didn't think it was possible, but now I do."

He was silent for a moment, still save for the slight tapping of his hand against his leg, and Anne realized he was regaining control of himself.

"Christopher—"

"Do you really think that any wife of mine would set foot on stage?"

"What?"

"After all that happened, you still have the thought in your mind that you would act or sing again in such a public forum?" he asked, before sighing and softening his voice and his words. "You have a beautiful voice, Anne, and I would love nothing more than to hear it again. But you must realize that the wife of an earl cannot be seen taking part in such a — *profession*."

"And do you seriously believe that I would let any husband of mine control me so?" she asked, narrowing her eyes, and as they stared at one another, she realized they were at an impasse. She looked around her, suddenly, remembering where they were, the number of people who surrounded them. Most villagers continued on their way with watchful eyes and the odd stare, and Anne rubbed at her forehead, right beside where her scar still slightly itched.

"We are getting nowhere," Christopher finally said, his hands on his hips as he followed her gaze, looking around them. "This is a courtship, Anne, so it is the time to get to know one another to … figure things out. Let's talk this through when we are somewhere quieter, when we have each had time to think things through."

He looked at her expectantly, apparently still believing that she would change her mind, that once she had time to consider his position, she would do as he wished. Well, he had a surprise coming. But she agreed that now was not the time to argue, especially when they had just come back to one another. And so she nodded, took his arm, and walked with him out of the village.

CHAPTER 17

Christopher made his way through the impressive, richly appointed hallways of Longhaven, feeling Breckenridge's ancestors staring down at him, as though they were judging the man who would potentially marry one of their own. Would he? Should he? He had thought Anne had changed. He still wanted her to be the happy, wonderful, free spirit she always had been — just with a little more restraint, perhaps. Could a person not follow the expectations set out for her and still maintain her character?

With his mind in turmoil, he entered one of the drawing rooms with a frown on his face. The opulent, burgundy room, its walls and ceilings painted by a master, was both impressive and intimidating, though which he wasn't sure. His own home was fine, but not as extensive — all semblance of thought came to a halt when he saw Anne. She stunned him, every time he saw her. Whether she had dressed so exquisitely for him or not, he didn't know, but she wore a gown of shimmering blue, which perfectly set off her eyes, the matching blue ribbon striking in her blonde hair.

"Anne," he breathed, and when he saw the corners of her

eyes crinkle and her mouth break into a smile, only then did he realize that Breckenridge and his mother were also in the room, staring at him in some disbelief. He cleared his throat. "That is, *Lady* Anne," he said with a slight bow to her as well as Lady Cecelia. "You look lovely this evening. As do you, Your Grace. Breckenridge," he added with a nod.

"Do I not look lovely as well?" his friend asked in laughter.

Christopher's cheeks burned, but he chuckled in spite of himself as he stepped forward. Anne rose from her place and took him by the arm, leading him to the small settee in the corner.

"Christopher," she said softly so that only he could hear. "I just wanted to apologize today. I was wrong for arguing with you. I want you to know that marrying you would not be a hardship, and would, in fact, be of equal status to me as returning to the stage. A person can have more than one passion."

Thinking on the importance his own land and people held for him, he nodded in understanding.

"I suppose that makes sense," he said. "I realize how difficult this has all been for you." Especially giving up the stage, though he was glad to learn that she would no longer be holding out a hope to return.

They rejoined the conversation with her family, the four of them in good spirits when the butler appeared at the door.

"Your Grace," he said politely but with some urgency, and they all turned to him expectantly. "You have visitors. Lord Rumsfelter and his wife, Lady Gertrude."

"This is a surprise," Lady Cecelia said, turning to Breckenridge, who nodded in agreement. "They were at the Wintertons' house party," she added. "Perhaps they are stopping through on their return home?"

Perhaps, thought Christopher, though he was concerned

at the timing, which seemed a bit too coincidental. He had hoped the news of Anne's scandal had not yet made its way to the country. But if that was where it had originated, there was no reason, of course, that it had not made its rounds among the elite outside of London as well. He liked Rumsfelter well enough, but he knew the man's wife was something of a gossip.

"Show them in," said Breckenridge with some resignation, and Christopher took Anne's arm and spoke low in her ear.

"Anne," he murmured, "there is something you should know."

"What?" She turned to him with concern in her eyes, and as much as it broke his heart, he opened his mouth to tell her that her story was no longer a secret, but the couple entered the room before he could say a word.

"Ah, your grace. Lady Cecelia. Lady Anne," said Lady Rumsfelter, whose face was wreathed in demure smiles, but Christopher could detect something more at play in the way her eyes settled on Anne. "Oh, and Lord Merryweather, how lovely to see you again."

"Lady Rumsfelter," he said, inclining his head, as did the rest of them.

"My apologies for surprising you so, Breckenridge," said Lord Rumsfelter, who had the courtesy to look somewhat embarrassed at their unwarranted visit. "We were returning home, and Lady Rumsfelter was so worried about Lady Anne and her sudden disappearance from the Winterton house party that she said she simply had to stop in."

"Well, you must stay for dinner," Breckenridge said, but Lord Rumsfelter held up his hand. "No, no."

"We insist," said the Dowager Duchess, and Lady Rumsfelter clapped her hands together in glee. "Oh, how lovely, thank you!"

"I will go speak with Cook, Your Grace," the butler said

from the doorway, bowing and departing, leaving them alone.

"Oh, Lady Anne!" Lady Rumsfelter said rushing over to her. "Your poor face! Whatever happened?"

"I had an accident," Anne said politely, though Christopher could see the stiffness in her spine.

"Oh?" Lady Rumsfelter raised one perfect eyebrow. "Oh my, what sort of accident?"

"An item fell on me from high above," Anne said softly but with an air of finality.

Christopher loved the way she coupled honesty with evasion. Loved? The word gave him a jolt. Where had that come from? And when had he ever enjoyed any sort of duplicity?

"An item?" said Lady Rumsfelter with a sly grin, "or a hook?"

"Excuse me?" Anne said, while Lord Rumsfelter walked over and put a hand on his wife's arm. "That's enough, Gertrude."

"I'm so sorry," Lady Rumsfelter said, placing a hand over her heart. "That was careless of me. I am simply still in shock over what I was told, though I am so sorry to hear what happened to you Lady Anne. Oh, Lord Merryweather, before I forget, Lady Patricia, the eldest of the Winterton girls, said if I were to see you to give you her well wishes. She had hoped to have the chance to say farewell to you before you returned home, though she looks forward to your reacquaintance in London for the season."

Christopher simply nodded, though he came to stand behind Anne as he felt she needed solidarity at the moment. Smiling, he took her arm as they were called into dinner.

* * *

BECAUSE THE EARL LOVED ME

ANNE HAD ALWAYS HATED Gertrude Danting. Ever since they were girls, the woman had it out for her. They had come out the same season, and Anne had always garnered much more attention than Gertrude, though Gertrude had gloated over her when she had been married her first season out.

That she would come here, today — and bait Christopher, of all things! Clearly, the woman knew what had happened to her, and if she knew, that meant most of the *ton* would as well. How had it gotten out? She sighed. It didn't matter, really. Not anymore, at least to her.

She took her seat and was pleased when Christopher sat beside her. She hadn't been sure how he would feel about the fact that there was now scandal attached to her name, but that he was standing by her meant more to her than she could have said.

They had just begun the first course when Gertrude started in again.

"Anne, I was so worried for you." Anne rolled her eyes.

"Did you just roll your eyes at me?"

"Yes, Gertrude, I did," she said, putting her soup spoon down, not caring any longer for societal niceties. What did it matter? This woman hadn't broken any conventions, but Anne would have preferred she simply told her the true reason she was here — that she wanted to collect gossip to share with others so they could laugh at Anne behind her back. "You were not worried about me. You have never cared about me. In fact, you were probably happy to hear that my face has been ruined."

"Anne!" her mother admonished, and she sensed Christopher cringe beside her.

"Well, it's true," she said, looking around at all of them. "What would you like me to say? To lie through my teeth like Gertrude here? Say what you'd like to say, Gertrude, and be done with it."

Gertrude put down her own utensils and leaned forward.

"Fine, Anne," she said with a sneer. "You've got what was coming to you. You've always pushed convention, and now you did something so stupid, so childish, that you are finally suffering some consequences. I'm glad you were hurt, as now, perhaps, you have learned your lesson. You are the daughter of a duke, for God's sake! Although, now we know you will never be the wife of any respectable peer, not with you looking like that and with everyone knowing the scandal you have brought on yourself and your entire family."

Anne's chest constricted. She knew she had asked for this, but to actually hear the words aloud was another matter entirely.

"I — I—"

Pretend you are a heroine, Anne. You are Joan of Arc, except your enemy has much more venom and bite.

She opened her mouth, but before she could say anything, she was shocked into silence.

"Actually," Christopher said, placing a hand over hers, "Lady Anne will soon become a countess."

"What?" Anne realized it was her own voice that questioned him, though all of the heads at the table swiveled toward him.

"Lady Anne and I are to be married," he said, looking at her with a reassuring smile, "as soon as possible, in fact."

"Oh," Gertrude said, seeming somewhat deflated. "Con-congratulations."

Anne didn't even look at her. She could think of nothing but Christopher, who had just taken one of the most impulsive actions she had ever witnessed in her entire life.

* * *

BECAUSE THE EARL LOVED ME

No one was more shocked by his announcement than Christopher himself. He hadn't meant for the words to come out, hadn't yet decided whether marrying Anne was the right path to take, but when Lady Rumsfelter had begun to disparage her, saying such vicious things to her, despite the fact that Anne had asked for it, Christopher hadn't been able to listen to it any longer. He had needed to let this woman know that Anne was so much more than all the terrible things Lady Gertrude had accused her of.

And so he had let the first thing that came into his mind cross his lips. Lady Rumsfelter had recovered rather admirably and she continued to look from one of them to the other as though determining where the weak point was from which to launch her attack. What Lady Rumsfelter didn't realize, however, was that she had united them against her, and anything she said would be fended off by the two of them, a force that was stronger than even they had realized.

Anne's mother, who before had looked rather distraught, now sat tall in her chair, a wide smile on her face. Clearly, she was pleased, and Breckenridge simply looked relieved. He gave Christopher a nod of thanks, then returned to his dinner plate in front of him.

Lord Rumsfelter was simply flummoxed. The rest of the dinner passed in abrupt silence and stilted conversation, and the couple took their leave the second the dessert plates were cleared, any societal niceties that had been present now completely vanished.

"Farewell," Lady Rumsfelter said as she walked from the room, "this has been so … enlightening. I will be sure to tell everyone the good news. Do give my best to the Duchess."

And with that, they were gone, leaving a silent, tense room behind them.

"Well," said Breckenridge, pushing his chair back from the

table, "I believe the two of you have much to discuss. Why don't you take a moment in the drawing room?"

"I shall accompany you," said the Dowager Duchess, rising. "How exciting. We shall—"

She stopped at Breckenridge's outstretched hand. "Give them a moment, Mother."

"But—"

"Please."

And so Christopher stood, held his arm out to Anne, and led her out of the dining room as he tried to determine what in the hell he was going to say to her. He had only a few steps to figure it out.

CHAPTER 18

Anne settled herself on the velvet settee while Christopher slowly eased into the beige tufted club chair across from her. He looked agitated, she thought, tilting her head to the side, not knowing whether to laugh or be concerned.

"Christopher, are you all right?" she finally said, and he nodded quickly.

"Of course, just fine," he said, though he had a slightly panicked look in this eyes. "Anne—"

"Christopher, I understand."

"What do you mean?"

"You don't have to marry me — at least, not right away."

"I said I would, and therefore I will." His tight grip on the arms of the chair told her that he was not altogether pleased about their conversation.

"I know you said that to Gertrude in my defense, and for that, I will be forever grateful," Anne said, leaning toward him. "But I do not want you making what you feel is a mistake because of that. I only want you to marry me if that truly is your desire, not because you feel you have an obligation to do so. I know that to marry immediately would be rather ... sudden for you."

He was silent for a moment — too long a moment for Anne.

She sighed. "It's all right, Christopher."

He stood and walked over to the window, peering out into the darkness. "It is not all right."

"You must be in turmoil," she said, raising herself and walking over to him, coming behind him and placing a hand on his arm. His head tilted down toward her touch, but other than that he had no reaction. "I know such an impulsive decision does not come easily for you," she continued. "I appreciate your words — truly, I do — but I am offering to put you out of your misery."

He raised his eyebrows. "You are going to kill me?"

"No!" She laughed, encouraged by the ghost of a smile playing around his lips. "I am giving you a choice — one last decision, as it were. We courted, then didn't, and are now courting again. We seem to be going back and forth and running circles around one another. Tomorrow, Christopher, you will be returning home. At least, that was your plan. You said you wanted to be with me, but now that this decision has been foisted upon you, I see how difficult you are finding it. All I ask is that, before you go, you must tell me, one way or the other, if you would like me in your life or not. Is that fair?" Even as she said the words, her heart broke thinking of the possibility of him leaving her, but this had to be said.

"More than fair," he said, his voice echoing off the windowpane.

He turned, started a bit at her closeness, but then pulled her toward him.

"Anne," he said gently, running a hand down her cheek, the scarred one. "You were rather forward with that woman, you know that. Much more forward than you should have been." She bit back a retort when he held up a finger. "I know what you're going to say," he continued, "she deserved it. And very well, she probably did. But my God, I have never witnessed a scene like that, especially among polite company." He sighed. "What she said, though, Anne, you must know, was simply not true. She was only trying to hurt you. You are beautiful. You are like ... sunshine. And everyone who knows you is better for it."

He kissed her then, a simple kiss, but one that made her heart fill with hope that maybe — just maybe, he could love her for exactly who she was.

* * *

THIS WOMAN WAS GOING to be the death of him, Christopher thought the next morning.

She teased him, she attracted him, and she scared the hell out of him. Life with her would be an adventure, and Christopher was not the adventurous type. Far from it. He needed to get his mind set, to think things through in an orderly fashion. She had given him until tonight to decide, and now in the morning light's freshness, he was going to determine exactly what it was he should do.

Thinking on the disastrous dinner of the previous evening, Christopher found Breckenridge's library, sitting down with his usual cup of coffee at the writing desk in the corner, a blank sheet of paper and quill pen in front of him.

Whenever a decision needed to be made, Christopher found there was one method of thinking that helped him to decide. He would make a list of the positive and negative aspects of following through on the potential course of action.

He made a "+" on one side of the page, a "-" on the other, and drew a line down the middle. He tapped the pen on his cheek and considered the paper in front of him.

The negatives came rather quickly.

Disorder. Lack of sense. Scandal. More scandal. For he didn't think Anne would be limited to one. *Dramatics. Broken plans. Disregard for propriety.*

Finished for the moment, he looked to the paper's other side and finally wrote one word. *Anne.*

He didn't know how long he sat there, staring at the long list on one side and the four letters on the other. Could one truly outweigh all of the others? He was flummoxed. His mind told him one thing, but his heart was reaching the other way.

"Christopher!"

He turned at Anne's cry, seeing her framed in the doorway, dressed today in a sunny yellow dress that seemed to reflect her spirits.

"Come quickly! Ella is here!"

Bloody hell.

* * *

HE FOLLOWED Anne down the long corridor, watching her rush into the room where the butler gestured. Anne embraced Ella, but as Christopher stood at the drawing room's entrance, just out of sight, the horror of the day he had met the woman came rushing back to him. When he had seen Anne hit by that hook, he hadn't even known if she was alive.

Now, the arrival of this woman brought it all back — the guilt, the horror, and the pain.

He must have moved, for the eyes of both Anne and Ella were soon trained on him where he stood in the doorway.

"Lord Merryweather!" Ella said, coming over to him with a small, hesitant smile. "How lovely to see you again. You did marvelous work caring for Anne's wound, I see. Why it's nearly healed already!"

He didn't acknowledge her words as she curtsied to him.

"What are you doing here?" he asked, ignoring Anne's hiss of disapproval from across the room.

"Oh," Ella's cheeks turned pink. "I — I'm sorry. We were in the area, and Anne said to call and well..." Her voice dropped. "I needed somewhere to go. Things have gotten fairly ... conflicted with the theatre, and I am worried something may happen."

"What do you mean?" Christopher asked. He had seen far too much of the theatre company, and as much as he would prefer Ella hadn't chosen Anne as the person to turn to, he certainly wouldn't wish any ill upon her. She was a decent sort and had been there when Anne was in need. She simply reminded him of all that had gone wrong, of all that *could* go wrong in the future. Did she even realize she was in the home of a duke?

"Kitty has become more vocal of the fact that she wants all of the lead parts and if she should not get one, well, she will make sure that the winning lady is not able to perform her task," she said, despair etched on her face. "You saw what happened to Anne. We are returning to London soon and will put on Romeo and Juliet, and I have been given the part of Juliet. Kitty was livid. We have a few days' break after our performance in Chatham, and I figured I was best to spend it somewhere away from them until I determine what I am to do."

"Of course you can stay here!" Anne said, flinging her arms around her friend, and Christopher sighed. She *would* say that. Well, at the very least, they were still at Breckenridge's home and that meant his friend would have to deal with it. It was the perfect time for Christopher to take his leave.

As he approached Anne to tell her of his departure, Breckenridge himself walked into the room, a piece of paper in hand.

"Ah, good, you are all here," he said. "And you must be Miss Anston. Thank you for all you did for my sister."

Breckenridge, the damn charmer.

"Now, then, to the task at hand! You will be pleased, Merryweather, with what my man brought with him upon his return this morning."

"Oh?"

"Your special license!"

"Special license?"

"Yes! For your marriage."

"You're getting married?" Ella's excited squeal overtook the room, and Anne turned to him, hope on her face.

"Oh, Christopher, you have decided then? Oh, I'm so glad!" she held her hands in front of her as if in prayer and tipped her face up to the heavens. "I was so worried that you would say no, that you wouldn't want me anymore. And a special license — we can get married nearly immediately! Alastair, how quickly do you think you can get the vicar? When shall we have the wedding? I must go tell Mother."

With that, she fled from the room, leaving Christopher standing there, completely and truly flummoxed.

"Ah…" Breckenridge said, looking at him with a bit of concern. "Was I a bit presumptuous?"

Christopher tried to stretch his mouth into a smile, but he could barely choke the words out. "No …. not at all."

* * *

BECAUSE THE EARL LOVED ME

CHRISTOPHER TWISTED his aching neck from one side to the other, cracking it as he sat on the edge of his bed, wondering if he would ever be able to sleep. The tension in his shoulders was stiff and unyielding. His sister had always said it was because he held himself so rigidly all the time.

"Just let go, Christopher," Ruth would say, "enjoy your life."

He smiled ruefully and shook his head. If only it were that easy. His sister, older than him by five years, had married some time ago and lived in the northern part of England, some ways away. He tried to see her once a year or so and did enjoy her brood of children, although being around them was complete chaos.

If only she could see him now, he chuckled. He must write to her soon and tell her all that had happened. Once he himself knew exactly what was in store for him, that was.

He wasn't quite sure how he had gotten himself into this situation. It seemed every time he tried to distance himself from Anne — from this entire family — he was somehow pulled back in.

And now Breckenridge had this license. Christopher sighed as he lay back, staring up at the ceiling. The mural in his room depicted a brood of angels, he thought, or maybe it was supposed to be cupid — he wasn't really sure. Well, it seemed there wasn't much choice now, despite what his plans had been for a courtship and betrothal. He had skipped over that part and would be a married man shortly.

He closed his eyes, willing himself to sleep when suddenly all of his senses rose in awareness. The door creaked, followed by the soft patter of feet. He smelled her before he opened his eyes to see her. Nothing else smelled like that — her unique blend of rosewater and lemon. Besides that, who else would sneak into his room in the dead of night?

"Christopher?"

Damnation.

CHAPTER 19

*A*nne hoped he couldn't hear the nervousness in her voice. She knew this was a risk, that she should turn around and go back the way she came, to her own bedchamber, where she should be simply dreaming of this and not actually acting it out. But she had to know the way of it.

After Alastair's announcement and their dinner the previous night, Anne had spent some time with Ella. She told her of all that had happened since she last saw her in Tonbridge, of Christopher's rescue and his subsequent stay at their home. Ella had been intrigued. "Why, it could be a play of its own!" she said, her fingers over her mouth.

"I suppose that is true," Anne said with a wry grin. "Though we have yet to know whether it will be a romance or a tragedy. Either way, I suppose it's a comedy of sorts."

"Oh, Anne, do not be silly," Ella said. "That man loves you."

"*Loves* me? Oh, I think not, Ella. I can tell you he feels something for me — perhaps affection, certainly desire — but I'm not sure he could ever love someone like me. In truth, I believe he despairs of me."

"I think you are being dramatic," Ella replied, her eyebrows raised. "Tell me, Anne, what do you feel for him?"

"I feel ... like I am falling in love with him," she said, dropping her head into her hands with an exaggerated moan. "Oh Ella, I shouldn't, I really shouldn't. But the more I am with him, the more I *want* to truly be with him. And I want even more than that. I wish I no longer had to worry about whether he may leave or whether he may find another. I want to go where he does, to be the only woman he has eyes for. Is that not ridiculous?"

"Not at all," Ella said, placing a hand on her knee. "I think it is lovely and I think you should tell him all that you just told me."

"Oh, but I couldn't," Anne said, shaking her head. "What if he were to turn me away? Or to tell me that he feels nothing of the sort for me, that he never will? I couldn't bear it."

"So instead, you will live your life unsure of what his feelings are?" Ella asked, raising an eyebrow. "I believe that would be all the worse, Anne."

"I need him to love me for me," she whispered, finally coming to the truth of the matter. "And I simply do not know if that is possible."

"There is only one way to be sure," Ella said with a pointed look, and Anne sighed in resignation, understanding her words. "Go to him," Ella urged, "ask him how he feels."

"Now?"

"Yes, now," she said with a laugh.

"But he is likely abed by now!"

"So?" Ella asked coyly, and Anne bit her lip, her cheeks warming at the thought. Would he be completely scandalized if she came to him? What would he do? It was not at all something Christopher would approve of, she thought as she let herself into her chamber. But sleep proved elusive. All she could do was pace her room, her heart in turmoil, before finally realizing she had to do as Ella said. She had to know.

So now here she was. She had thrown her wrapper over her nightgown. It was lace, one that would be better suited for a courtesan, she knew, but when she had seen it, she had to have it, and she'd had a secret conversation with the modiste. Her mother could never know. It was for no one but herself — or at least, it had been — so what did it matter? A bit of extravagance now and then was no sin.

But this was, was it not? To come to a man's bedchamber in the middle of the night?

"Anne."

Her name came off his lips huskily, and he turned over in bed to face her, the classic features of his face contorted.

"Are you all right?" she asked him, suddenly concerned.

"You really shouldn't be here," he said, pushing back the blankets slightly and sitting up.

"Oh!" she gasped. "Where is your shirt?"

"I don't wear one," he said, and apparently seeing her surprise, he shrugged. "I get warm at night."

Anne would never have guessed that a man like Christopher Anderson would sleep without any clothing. She had expected to find him in the most sensible nightshirt, a cap on his head, as she was told most gentlemen wore — for she hadn't seen any in such a state of undress, of course.

"Turn around, Anne," he said, his voice gruff, and for once in her life she obeyed, her heart beating fast as she wondered at what she was supposed to do now. All that she had planned to say to him — her soliloquy, as it were — had flown from her mind, her lines lost when she had caught sight of the well-defined muscles of his bare chest.

"You can turn back now," he said, and when she swiveled back to face him, he was now dressed in a nightgown, black and brown vertical stripes covering it, with black fur trim around the collar. She pulled her own dressing gown tighter around herself. His hands were in his pockets as a ravaged look crossed his face while he stared at her, which she didn't understand at all. Was he that upset that she had come to him so improperly?

"I — shouldn't have come," she said, taking a step back.

"No, you really shouldn't have," he sighed. "But you're here now, so you might as well tell me why."

Buck up, Anne. You have more courage than this.

She took a step forward this time, coming within a few feet of him, too nervous to go any closer.

"Christopher," she began, "I know all has happened rather quickly. When Alastair procured the special license, I thought that meant you had decided you wanted to be married to me, but upon your silence throughout dinner this evening, I realized that perhaps I was being somewhat presumptuous in my excitement. Would that be the case?"

His eye twitched, and he looked away from her, not quite meeting her gaze.

"I, ah … believe there may have been somewhat of a misunderstanding."

Her heart fell. It was as she had thought once she had taken a moment to think things through. "I see," she tried to keep all emotion out of her voice, despite the thick ball of it that seemed to clog her throat. "Very well then. I will tell Alastair that he should tell the vicar not to bother. Go home tomorrow, Christopher. I would wish for nothing more than to be your wife, but not if I am not wanted."

"Not wanted?" he said, his eyes catching hers, his expression incredulous. "Is that what you think? That I do not want you?"

"Well, of course," she said, confused now. Goodness, this man was contrary.

"Anne," he said, moving closer to her, and her heart beat

faster with every step he took. "Never think I do not want you. For I want you very, very much." He stood directly in front of her now, his hands reaching out to her, pulling her toward him so that their bodies were touching. "You are the most beautiful woman I have ever met. I have always thought so. Many would tell you that your eyes are the most shocking blue, the color of an aquamarine jewel. But that wouldn't do them justice. No, they are the color of the sky on a clear day, when the clouds have vanished and the sun has lit every part of the earth. For that is what your spirit is like. You make others around you feel the happiness you exude in equal measure."

A sound bubbled from her lips, half-sob, half-laughter.

"I realize I am rather dramatic."

He chuckled.

"That would be something of an understatement. But life is certainly not dull with you in it."

"You are also wrong about one thing," she said in a whisper. "I was beautiful, but I ruined that."

He leaned in and kissed her face, beside where the scar was healing.

"Every mark on our bodies tells the story of who we are," he said, his gaze intent on hers. "I know this holds memories that you would prefer to forget. But, instead, think of the good that came out of it. You know now that you can use your gift — that people love to listen to you, are held in rapture by your voice. You made a friend as ... controversial as she may be. And it allowed us to better get to know one another."

"Although it almost broke us apart as well."

"It did," he said, nodding, "that much is true."

"And now?" she asked, looking up at him. "What do you want now?"

He groaned slightly, so low she almost didn't hear it, and

he muttered something under his breath. Why was he forever doing that? She wanted to know his thoughts, and she hated straining to hear him.

"What was that?"

"I said I want you," he ground out, and he finally kissed her then, seizing her mouth with reckless abandon. Oh, she loved this side of him, the side that he so rarely allowed free reign. It struck her that she was likely one of the few people who had the privilege to have seen it. The thought filled her with a sense of satisfaction. Nearly equal to the satisfaction that came over her as Christopher began to kiss his way down her neck. He opened a button at the top of her gown, his fingers rather deft as he made his way to the bottom, following his hands with his lips.

When he opened the front of it to look at her, his eyes widened so far that she nearly laughed.

"What are you wearing?" he asked, his mouth open.

"A nightrail," she said with what she hoped was a demure shrug and a coy smile.

"I have never seen a lady wear a nightrail like that," he said.

"Good," she replied with a smile. "I shouldn't like to think of you with another woman in such a garment. Or any garment, were I being honest. Or none, or — I don't know what I am saying any longer."

He grinned wickedly at her, setting her nerves on edge. Oh, she more than liked this side of Christopher. She loved it very, very much.

Anne gasped in surprise as one of his arms came under her knees, and he picked her up bodily and tossed her on the bed.

"Christopher!" she said with a laugh, though she was enjoying this more than she could say. He eased one arm, then the other, out of her robe and ran his hands down the

BECAUSE THE EARL LOVED ME

sheer front of her nightrail to where the lace began. He fingered it gently before looking up at her.

"I think I like this," he said, raising an eyebrow as he looked at her, and now it was her turn to laugh at the enjoyment in his voice.

"I'm glad," she said breathily, "for I am not getting rid of it."

His hand came to one of her breasts, and when he fondled it reverently, she nearly came off the bed. He seemingly sensed her pleasure, for he rolled one of her nipples between his index finger and thumb, and she murmured his name, which apparently emboldened him all the more as he found her neglected breast and gave it the same treatment, while he replaced his hand with his mouth on her right side.

She gasped in shock — she hadn't realized this was part of the love act. No one had told her about *this*. In fact, Anne didn't know much about the whole of it. She understood it all in a sense, at least the very idea of it. It was in many of the stories and plays she saw or read, but nothing really described in detail what happened. It seemed she was about to find out.

Anne grasped Christopher's head in her fingers, running her hands through his silky brown locks, noting with some part of her mind that still functioned that his hair curled slightly at the ends. He must wet it down, she thought, and couldn't understand why he would control it when it was so beautiful as it was naturally.

Her focus returned to Christopher and his actions, as he was now slowly beginning to inch his way down her body.

"Christopher?" she asked, both intrigued and concerned. "Where are you going?"

He didn't answer her but began to lightly tug up the hem of her nightrail, being careful with the fragile fabric. He inched it up slowly, higher and higher, exposing more of her to his eyes. He ran his hands up her legs, which she knew were a little too long and a little too slim, but he didn't seem to mind. She shivered at the friction created by his palms as they went back and forth, each time inching higher and higher, until they were nearly at her very center. Was he going to enter her now, she wondered? She hadn't precisely come here for this — she had wanted to talk, though she wasn't stupid when she realized what a man might assume when a woman, particularly his — potential — betrothed, showed up in his bedchamber in the middle of the night. She supposed if they *were* to be married soon, did it really matter? Although, she thought, chewing her lip, in all the ways that she was so inappropriate, somehow waiting until her marriage night was important to her.

Suddenly, however, all thought stopped as Christopher's hand went as high as possible, finding her nub, and beginning to rub it back and forth.

She had to cover her mouth with her hand to keep from crying out, and anticipation built inside of her with a ferocity she could never have named.

"Oh, Christopher," she gasped, and as her pulse began to pound, she closed her eyes to enjoy what was to come, when suddenly she felt something much wetter, much more smooth upon her. She opened her eyes and looked down, both horrified and thrilled in equal measure.

"What are you doing?" she hissed, but he reached a hand up to interlock his fingers with hers, and before she could think any further, waves of bliss began to course through her. There was no way, really, to describe the feeling, the fire that shot through all of her limbs, radiating out beyond her fingers and toes, and when it was over, she was nearly numb from the experience.

When she finally came back to herself, lying replete on

the bed, she turned her head to see Christopher now on his knees, tidying her nightgown and smoothing her wrapper.

"Is — is that all?" she said, finding it almost difficult to speak.

He smiled at her.

"That is all for tonight," he said, though he seemed a bit agitated as he said it.

"But—"

"But nothing. I've gone far beyond what I should have, and there are some things that must remain." He cupped her cheek with his hand, and her face burned as she remembered what he had just done with those hands. "It seems as though I will be the lucky recipient of your marriage night, Anne, and we are not far away. You will simply have to wait until then. But let this be a reminder that you are beautiful, and you are wanted. Now you best go."

He held out her red dressing gown, and she slipped her arms into it. He helped her button the front and then turned her toward the door.

"Until the morning," he said in her ear and kissed her on the cheek before opening the door and sending her on her way.

CHAPTER 20

Christopher was having a difficult time eating breakfast the next morning, and all because of the woman sitting across from him. Every time he looked up, she caught his eye, giving him a small, knowing smile. When she stood to move to the sideboard, he knew she very purposely walked around his side of the table, allowing her dress to whisper across his back ever so slightly, with just enough contact to set him on edge.

He tried not to react, to show that nothing was amiss. And then her friend walked in.

"Good morning!" Ella said in a singsong voice, and as she sat down next to Anne, she looked at Christopher with a grin so wide that he knew without being told that Anne had confided in her. Bloody hell. He looked at Anne with what he hoped was a very telling glare, but she simply giggled and dug into her eggs.

"Is someone going to tell me what is going on here, or am I to be left in the dark?" Breckenridge finally said as he lifted his coffee to his mouth.

"Oh, Alastair," Anne said, waving her hand exuberantly

through the air. "It is nothing at all. Simply silly wedding preparations I have been speaking to Lord Merryweather about.

Ella let out a bit of a snort, and even Anne now shot her a look of consternation. Thank heaven Anne's mother hadn't come downstairs as of yet, Christopher thought.

When the interminable breakfast was finally over, Christopher asked Anne if he might speak to her for a moment in the gardens. Breckenridge nodded his approval, but told Anne to take her maid, though from the look he gave the two of them, he was clearly aware that perhaps it was too late for that.

"Do you remember the last time we were here?" Anne asked with a grin as she looked up at him, and he couldn't help but laugh.

"Of course," he said. "I shall never forget it. Our foray into the pond."

"Most gentlemen would not have been so understanding," she said. "And I thank you for it. In fact, I thank you for accepting me as I am. I realize that I am likely not the woman you thought I was or the woman you saw yourself taking as a wife. But you have been very understanding of my unconventional ways, and for that, I am forever grateful."

"Of course," he said, then pausing a moment before continuing. "Anne, why did you come to me last night?"

After she had left, he had realized that when she came to him, it was not for physical reasons, as much as he knew she had enjoyed it. That had only happened because he had lost control, had been unable to keep himself from her. When she'd entered his room, she had been slightly nervous, and there had clearly been something on her mind.

"Oh, you answered my question," she said, her fingers running along the petals of the flowers that remained in the garden boxes.

"Which was?"

"Whether you felt anything for me," she said. "I needed to know, for I wasn't going to go ahead with marriage without it. You showed me you wanted me, Christopher, but it went further than that. You cared solely about me, saw only to my needs, and I didn't even think about it until after."

She stopped and caressed his face with her fingers as she had the flower petals.

"Thank you." She stood on her toes and brushed a chaste kiss on his mouth.

"Christopher, there is something else I wanted to speak to you about," she said slowly. "When we spoke in the village, I told you I might like to return to the stage. I have been speaking with Ella and—"

"Lady Anne! Oh, Lady Anne!" Christopher had forgotten about Anne's maid, who was now running to them as quickly as she could in her serving clothes. "Her Grace is beginning to have the baby. She is asking for you."

"But it's too soon!" she exclaimed. "The accoucheur is not set to arrive for another day."

"The monthly nurse is with her," the maid said. "And your friend — Miss Anston — she is determined to enter, but the nurse will not allow her in. She wanted your thoughts first."

"I'm coming!" said Anne with a nod before turning to him. "Christopher, can we continue this conversation later?"

"Of course," he said. "Might I ask why the Duchess is in the country for the birth? Would it not have been far better to be in London?"

Anne smiled. "Olivia never does anything that she is supposed to do. She didn't want all and sundry knowing about her condition and her business so she asked to be surrounded by family only. Oh! I must send for her mother and sister. Goodness — Alastair! He must be going mad. He

BECAUSE THE EARL LOVED ME

has been so worried. I will be back, Christopher, and I'll talk to you soon! I am to be an aunt!"

And with that, she picked up her skirts and ran back toward the house as fast as her feet would allow her on the stone walkway.

Christopher understood the importance of this moment, and would never want to take anything away from her, although he did wonder at her words. What had she meant, that she had been speaking with Ella? That wasn't a good sign. He sighed as he looked around him. Anne had said Olivia wanted only family and friends here, and with all that was going on, he thought it best that he now return home. If he had felt uncomfortable about his position among the household before, he certainly would now even more so. He would determine his next steps once all was well with Breckenridge and his family.

After last night, he certainly couldn't go back on his word. Like it or not — and he did, he continued to tell himself — this marriage was going ahead. Perhaps now, they would just have a little more time. That was all he wanted.

He entered the house, wrote a note to both Anne and her brother, and was on his way within the hour.

* * *

ANNE DIDN'T THINK she had ever felt such contentment as when the baby cooed in her arms, reaching up her hand to wrap the tiniest of fingers around Anne's thumb.

"Oh, Olivia," she said, tears coming to her eyes. "She is beautiful."

"Of course she is," Olivia said, looking over at her husband with tears of her own.

The labor had been blessedly quick. Anne had finally convinced the nurse to allow Ella entry, and between the two of them, they were able to support Olivia as she brought this little darling into the world. The baby's eyes were already the Finchley blue, and Anne smiled into them.

"We must introduce little Hannah to Christopher!" she exclaimed suddenly. "I'm afraid I left him rather abruptly in the gardens. Sally, will you find Lord Merryweather and ask him if he would like to come to visit?" she asked, and the maid shook her head.

"My apologies, my lady, but Lord Merryweather has returned home," she said.

"Oh," Anne said, as disappointment flooded her, "was the idea of a birthing too untoward for the perfectly proper Lord Merryweather?"

"I am unsure, my lady," the maid said uncomfortably. "But he asked that you receive this."

She handed her the piece of paper and Anne scanned it quickly.

Anne,

Forgive my departure, but I wanted to provide you time with your sister-in-law. Do give her my congratulations, and I look forward to reuniting with your family very soon.

At a time that is most convenient for you, please send me correspondence and I will arrange for a small, simple celebration with some of our friends and acquaintances to celebrate our betrothal. I would be quite pleased to welcome you to my home.

Yours,

Christopher

Anne smiled, forgiving Christopher's hasty departure in light of his note. This was so like him, she thought with a smile. He was now doing things his way — the proper, sure, carefully planned way. And she was completely fine with that. For that was who he was — the man she loved.

* * *

BECAUSE THE EARL LOVED ME

CHRISTOPHER WALKED around his grounds with a contented sigh. Everything was back to the way it should be. He had returned home, he had planned out his betrothal and marriage in a straightforward, conventional path, and he would soon be welcoming Anne to his estate.

He had been home for a week now, and he could hardly wait to see her again. When he thought of the night in his bedchamber, a glimmer of a smile played on his lips. She was exquisite. She was a siren. She was—

"My lord?"

Ah, yes. His steward.

"Yes, Ridgely, that would be fine," he said to the man, who was just as thorough and practical as Christopher himself. He trusted him explicitly. So much so, that he didn't even realize what the man had asked him, so lost he was in his dreams of Anne. He resolved to be more restrained.

"Very good, My Lord," he said, "and as for Tom Harrison, the tenant…"

Ridgely droned on about the practical day-to-day matters, and Christopher followed him down the path, nodding and agreeing with his assessments. He did not like to be away from matters of business for long, but he had somehow felt it was his duty to see Anne. Now, it would be his duty for the rest of his days.

When matters were finished, he went inside and found himself beginning to wander through the estate, which now felt rather empty. He didn't realize how alone he had been until he had lived for a time with another family. While their family was rather small as well, it was full of much love and laughter, and Christopher missed it. Perhaps he shouldn't have left. Perhaps he should have waited— no, this was for the best.

He found his way to his office, styled to his liking with maps and the odd portrait. He sat at his desk and pulled out a sheet of paper and his quill pen, ready to plan his betrothal party. It would be a small celebration, with only Anne's mother, of course, as a chaperone, as well as her friend, Lady Honoria, and he must invite Lord Watson. He wasn't sure if Breckenridge would be inclined to attend, but that was no matter. And, perhaps, the Wintertons? No, not the Wintertons. That wouldn't do at all. Lord and Lady Southam, he decided. Lady Southam was well acquainted with Olivia Finchley and she and Anne got on well. And perhaps the Duke and Duchess of Carrington. That would be all, he decided with a nod as he came to the bottom of the paper. Now all he had to do was wait for Anne's letter. How long would she take to contact him?

He tapped his fingertips on the chair, getting up and walking to the window. A sigh slipped out. Maybe he should simply go to her. That would be far—

"My lord?"

His butler approached. "Your correspondence."

Christopher picked it up eagerly, realizing he was no better than a schoolboy waiting for a love note. No matter. Ah! There it was. He picked up the envelope, breaking the seal and sliding the piece of paper out.

Christopher,

I am sorry you left so suddenly, but I look forward to seeing you once more and to celebrating our engagement. We hope to be there within the week.

Yours,

Anne

Within the week! He had much to do to prepare. Finally, everything was going his way.

CHAPTER 21

"Now, Mrs. Appleton, you have the menu set for the dinner tomorrow? I would like—"

"Aye, milord, I know what you like," said the Cook, who began to shoo him out of the kitchen. "Now, get going. Your bride will be here any minute. You want her to find you down here in the kitchens?"

"I'm sure she won't mind. I just wanted to be sure—"

"You can be sure. I've been doing this for your family for forty years, boy, and not much has changed in that time. Though I would never have caught sight of your father down here. Now off with you!"

He laughed at his cook. She still thought of him as the child he had been, the one she chased out of her kitchens when he came down to steal a piece or two of pie. He didn't know, however, what he would do without her.

Really, his nerves were on edge. Why, he had no idea. He had spent quite some time with Anne. Nothing had changed except for the fact that they were now doing this the right way.

"Fletcher, there you are!" He caught sight of his valet who, if he didn't know better, seemed to be trying to leave the room before Christopher saw him. "Fletcher, I have selected my clothing for the dinner tomorrow. I placed it on the bed. Did you find it? You must be sure it is pressed and ready well in advance."

"Yes, My Lord, all is in order."

"Are you sure? I would not want my guests to think I do not look altogether proper."

"I am sure, My Lord," Fletcher said, and Christopher wondered why his lips were pressed together so tightly. Surely he couldn't be upset that his employer took an interest in such matters? Christopher was the one who would be wearing the clothes, after all.

"Fletcher, have you seen Dibney or Mrs. Allen?" He should speak with the butler and housekeeper, to ensure that all of the rooms were made up and ready for his guests. He hadn't seen them in some time, he realized now.

"Ah, no, My Lord. Perhaps—"

But he never heard his valet's suggestion, as a loud crash arose from the foyer. "What in the hell…"

He started toward the noise but had barely made it to the entrance of Gracebourne's foyer when he was suddenly tackled by something small yet powerful.

"Christopher! Oh, Christopher, how I've missed you! I know it has only been a week, but I have so longed to see you. And a small party, how lovely!"

"Anne," he said, the smile stretching over his face. She was a force, this one, but suddenly the drab green walls seemed to brighten to mint, the lifeless portraits of his ancestors came to life, their frowns turning into grins. "I am very pleased to see you too."

"Oh, don't be so stoic," she said, stepping back from him and playfully swatting him on the arm. "I have so much to tell you! Olivia had the baby, and she is simply darling — the

BECAUSE THE EARL LOVED ME

baby that is, not Olivia. Although, Olivia is too, but that is not what I meant. Anyway, they are both doing wonderfully and I have never seen Alastair so happy before. He was very nervous, Christopher, you must have realized that. I told Olivia we would not stay away long, but of course, I wanted to see you again and celebrate with you. That was rather boorish of you to leave as you did, but I suppose you felt as though it was for our family to celebrate. But you must realize that you are now our family as well, do you not? Or you will be soon. That's right, I meant to ask you before the other guests arrived. When are we to be wed? Alastair seemed rather agitated about it before we left, but I told him not to worry — that I was sure you had a plan."

His head was slightly spinning by the speed and number of her words, which she had clearly been storing for quite some time. He took a moment to digest it all. He found she was looking at him expectantly.

"Yes, I do — have a plan that is," he said. "My original thought was that we wait until the season and be married in London, but that seems a bit too far away doesn't it?"

"That would be a few months still!" she said, and he laughed at how wide her eyes became.

"Yes, well, that was my thought as well," he said, sobering for a moment. "And I also considered that the sooner we married, the less talk there would be about all that happened to you. Perhaps by next month? I know your brother has the license, but then we could allow the banns to be read, and we could be married in the village church. What do you say? Would that be agreeable?"

She reached up and framed his face with her hands, which were cool on his skin.

"Yes," she said, softly kissing his lips, once, twice, three times, "it would be."

He was about to tell her that she couldn't very well kiss

him in the middle of the foyer, where staff would be coming and going, but at that moment he heard another voice fill the room.

"Oh, this house is simply divine, Anne! It could use a bit of color, to be sure, but the rooms are lovely. You should see the library and the views beyond. It is wonderful!"

Christopher went completely still as the woman walked into the room, a smile on her face as she twirled about her.

"Anne," he said quietly, "what is she doing here?"

"Oh!" she said, her hand coming to her mouth. "I forgot to tell you. Ella cannot return to the theatre company."

"What?"

"She heard from another actress that Kitty has made it clear that she plans to be rid of her, one way or the other. I wanted to go find Kitty and tell her what I thought, but Ella would not allow it. She said she will simply find another company. I don't agree, but well, this is Ella's decision. Anyway, she had nowhere to go, and I couldn't very well leave her with my brother, so she came here."

He sighed and rubbed his forehead, muttering to himself about the fact that some people just did not understand all of the intricacies that went into planning such an event. And this woman would not be accustomed to dining with the upper classes. Why, he had invited a duke and duchess! He groaned.

"Is something the matter Christopher?"

He looked up from the floor to catch her worried expression, and he pressed his lips together and shook his head. "Not at all," he managed, "where is your mother?"

"She is coming — ah, there she is."

Christopher greeted the Dowager Duchess, who excused herself quickly, saying she was exhausted from the travel. Christopher called out to a passing maid, who led her up the stairs to her room.

"Now then," he said, already rearranging his plan for the following day. "Let me go find my housekeeper to have her prepare another room."

* * *

ANNE WAS THRILLED when the guests began to arrive for the party. They were all lovely people, who she hadn't seen in some time. She wished Alastair and Olivia could attend, but of course, they would not return to parties and the like for some time. She had told Olivia she would wait to marry until she was ready to re-enter society, but Olivia had laughed at her and told her not to be silly — she said Anne couldn't hold back on her entire life because of her.

Anne was particularly glad to see Honoria.

"Oh, it's been far too long," Anne said as she embraced Honoria when she arrived with an older cousin in tow as a chaperone.

"It has, hasn't it? I know we've discussed everything in length through our letters, but I am so happy we finally have a chance to talk in person."

She took Anne's arm and began to walk with her through the foyer, ducking her head into various rooms to try to find one that suited what she was looking for.

"In here," Anne said, choosing a drawing room she had found earlier, one decorated in golds and crimsons that was welcoming.

"Anne, I was so worried," said Honoria, "I wanted to come after you with Lord Merryweather, I did, but it seems rather provident that I did not do so. Now, Anne, you must tell me of all that occurred and don't leave a bit of it out."

She brought a hand to the side of Anne's face, beside her scar. "Does it hurt much?"

"Not anymore," Anne replied, dipping her head. "It looks ghastly, doesn't it?"

"It truly is not so bad," said Honoria with a soft smile, taking Anne's hand in hers. "It adds character to your face."

She rolled her eyes at Anne's snort of laughter.

"Now as for Lord Merryweather," Honoria continued, "The last I saw you, you were trying to discourage his affections. Now here you are, betrothed."

And so, huddled in the drawing room of Christopher's home — soon to be hers, Anne supposed — she told Honoria the entire story. Honoria was quite the audience; gasping, crying, laughing when appropriate.

"My goodness, Anne," she said when Anne had finished. "I am so sorry for all the dreadful things that happened to you, but I must say, you certainly can tell a story, darling."

"Thank you," Anne said, pleased that she hadn't lost any of her skill.

At the chime from the long-case clock, Anne jumped up. "Oh, Honoria, I have been regaling you with tales for far too long. Come, we must join the others!"

The afternoon was a merry one, with the arrival of many guests. Anne looked around for Ella, but she had vanished. She supposed she had gone for her afternoon sleep, which she was used to from being awake until odd hours on the stage. All in all, Anne was quite looking forward to this celebration. Now all she needed to do was have Christopher remain agreeable — especially when she told him of the idea she and Ella had concocted.

* * *

CHRISTOPHER WATCHED her from across the room. Her smile was as bright as any lantern, her dress, a burnt orange that would have looked hideous on anyone but her, like the sun. A sun which everyone, most especially him, seemed to revolve around.

They had gathered in the drawing room, to prepare for the celebration dinner tonight. All was going to plan so far, Christopher noted with satisfaction. Miss Anston had not even joined them. When she did, he knew they might have to explain the entire, sordid story. His guests were polite enough not to say anything, but he could sense the curiosity nonetheless.

Anne didn't seem to mind, however, as she weaved between the guests, greeting them all with her friendly, lovely way. She was prone to dramatics, he knew that, but she was also equally adept at hostessing, which would be excellent when she took on the role of his countess.

"Lady Anne," he said, coming over to greet her. A jolt of heat burned through him when she turned her magnificent smile upon him.

"Lord Merryweather," she said, in turn, and the way she looked at him made him feel as though he were the only man in the room.

"You look beautiful this evening," he said, "as you always do."

"Thank you," she responded, with a slight curtsy, "you are too kind."

"I only tell the truth, love," he said.

The way her eyes danced at his words made his heart seem to skip a beat.

"Anne!" Honoria joined them. "Will you sing for us? It has been so long since I've heard your voice, and I truly miss it."

"I— I'm not sure," she said hesitantly, as though she was remembering the last time she had sung. She looked at Christopher.

"Please," he said, sweeping out his hand in front of him, as though clearing a stage for her.

"Very well," she said, though she was twisting her hands in her skirt nervously.

She wandered over to the pianoforte. Christopher had been contemplating ridding himself of the thing at one point, but he was glad he had kept it. It had been his mother's, and he hadn't been sure whether or not to hold onto it.

Anne began to play, and heads turned as all watched her, anticipating what was to come. No one was disappointed when the melody began to flow from her. Christopher could think of nothing but her, watching her as she tilted her head back, closed her eyes, and allowed the words and notes to flow. It was not a performance that would have been acceptable in most English drawing rooms. And yet, it didn't seem to matter here, as all were entranced.

Suddenly he was taken back to the theatre, to the moments before the hook had fallen. He remembered his thoughts then, as they were now. This was where she belonged, entertaining, using her voice to captivate others. What was he doing, holding her back from that?

She finally finished, a look of such contentment coming over her face. Could the rest of the party hear his heart beating through the wall of his chest?

CHAPTER 22

Anne drew the song to a close, relishing every last note. A sudden burst of applause overtook her from all sides, and she opened her eyes, astonished when she looked around and saw the gathered crowd.

"Oh!" she exclaimed with a laugh. "I had nearly forgotten you were all here! Thank you so much."

Her cheeks burned slightly as she stole a glance at Christopher. His gaze was hooded, unreadable, and an odd sensation built in her stomach.

The butler stepped into the room behind Christopher and whispered something to him before Christopher invited them all to come in for dinner. Anne walked over to him, and he held his arm out for her but didn't look at her, instead keeping his gaze straight ahead. What was wrong with him?

"Where is Ella?" Christopher murmured to Anne, and a bit of worry flitted through her as she realized it had been some time since she had seen her friend. She knew Ella was worried about her manners at such a dinner party, but Anne had done her best to coach her earlier in the day.

"I'm not sure," she whispered back, her brows coming together in a vee. "Do you suppose I should go check on her?"

"I'm sure she's fine," he reassured her. "Perhaps she felt awkward among us."

"And why would she feel awkward?" Anne asked, pulling her arm from him and placing her hands on her hips, despite the fact that Christopher was actually correct. "You didn't say anything to her, did you?"

"No," he shook his head, "of course not."

She eyed him warily, not quite trusting him, and he seemed a bit affronted. While it was true that he had never given her any cause to distrust him in the past, he certainly hadn't been very welcoming to Ella. She decided not to question him any further, and, letting the matter go, allowed him to pull out her chair and seat her.

Once everyone was around the table, Christopher cleared his throat and addressed them all. "We would like to thank all of you for coming. I know this is all rather ... unexpected, but we appreciate you being here to celebrate our upcoming union. Lady Anne—"

A commotion at the door interrupted his words, and the guests all turned. Ella was on the floor, trying to pick up what had been their first course. She must have entered at entirely the wrong time and crashed into the servant. The footman was now trying to wave her away to clean it himself, but Ella was insisting that she help him.

"It was entirely my fault," Ella said. "I was going too fast and not paying attention to where I was going, and I— oh dear. I am making things worse."

Anne turned to Christopher and, seeing his mouth open in shock as he stared at Ella, she put a finger on his chin to close his jaw. The poor woman was already embarrassed enough.

"Ella!" Anne called and pushed back her chair to walk over to her, taking her arm and lifting her to her feet. "I am so happy you could join us this evening."

"Yes, well..." She stood, and Anne saw that she was wearing what was likely the most hideous dress she had ever seen. Thank heavens Lady Rumsfelter wasn't here.

Anne pointed Ella to the remaining seat, whispering to her not to worry about the food. She looked at Christopher and saw his face had gone white, as he lifted his drink to his lips and took a long swallow.

Oh dear.

* * *

CHRISTOPHER HAD THOUGHT the dress Anne had worn onstage was bad, but this was truly awful. After Ella had finally taken her seat while the other guests politely conversed among themselves, Anne resumed her chair and Christopher leaned over to whisper in her ear, "Did you not think of giving her a dress to wear for the party?"

Anne lifted her shoulders and glared at him in defense of her friend.

"She said she had a dress."

"*That* does not qualify as a dress."

He didn't know if it could be called gold or yellow, but it was the color of old, aged mustard, and did nothing for Ella's complexion. In truth, despite the fact that she was actually a striking woman, she looked awful, and yet the gown's brightness made it hard to look anywhere else.

"Continue your speech," Anne hissed to him, as the footman came in with a replacement tray.

"Ah, yes," he said, clearing his throat once more and garnering the table's attention. "Lady Anne Finchley is a woman of many talents," he continued. "She loves to sing, to read, to be light and laughter to everyone she meets. Now, she will be taking on a new role — that of countess and my wife. I could not be a luckier man."

Anne smiled at him then, a true smile, and it made it hard to breathe for a moment. Until the clatter of a spoon broke the silence, and Christopher swung his head around to the offending noise.

"I'm sorry," Ella whispered. "I didn't realize we weren't to eat yet."

Christopher nodded tightly, feeling the tension begin to increase through his shoulders. He had hours of this still. He sorely wished Ella had stayed in her room tonight.

"It's fine," Anne said with a bright grin at her friend, "no problem at all. You haven't eaten all day and must be hungry. Go ahead."

Christopher tried to think of what he had meant to say next, but his thoughts were gone, replaced by his irritation with the woman without manners.

"Very well," he said instead. "Why do we not begin?"

"Anne," the Duchess of Carrington, Isabella Hainsworth, said, "Will you sing for us again after dinner? Your voice is simply marvelous."

"If you'd like," Anne replied, a smile crossing her face, and Ella nodded at her.

"She is divine, is she not, my lady?"

"Your Grace, Miss Anston," Christopher said quickly, hearing the disapproval in his voice at her misstep, but the Duchess waved her hand. "It is no problem at all, Miss Anston," she said. "Call me whatever you'd like. Isabella is fine."

"My apologies, Your Grace," Ella said, looking down at her plate, and for a moment, Christopher felt like something of a brute. At Anne's glare, he knew he needed to try harder to change his countenance, to understand where Ella was coming from. "And my apologies to you, My Lord."

"All is well," he said, resolutely, trying to convince himself that it was.

"Anyway," she continued. "All I wanted to say was how wonderful it will be when everyone, regardless of class, will be able to hear Anne's beautiful voice onstage once again."

"Excuse me?"

It was now Christopher's spoon that dropped to his plate, and he looked at Anne, questioning the veracity of Ella's words, hoping he wasn't understanding her correctly. Anne's cheeks had gone pink, her eyes wide, and her hands were twisting together in her lap.

"I— ah ... that is, I'm sorry, Anne, I thought he would have known by now," Ella said. "It's just that, Anne and I, we have decided to combine our talents, to forge ahead with a company of our own. We are going to travel—"

"Enough!" Christopher barely heard her words, unable to hear any more from Miss Anston. He had eyes and ears only for Anne, who was now looking at him beseechingly.

"Christopher—" she began, turning to him, but was quickly interrupted when the door swung open quickly.

"For the love of God!" he said, standing and throwing down his napkin, as in the entrance stood not a footman, nor Dibney his butler, but two actors from the company — one he recognized as the leading man who had coerced Anne away — Lawrence, she had said his name was, the other the woman Anne claimed had hurt her. "Get out of my house!" he commanded.

"I'm sorry, My Lord," Dibney said as he rushed in behind them, his typically immaculate hair askew after his apparent rush through the estate. "I tried to bar them entry but they pushed their way in. There is nothing I could do."

"It's all right, Dibney," he said, coming around the table in front of his guests — the guests who now stood staring, spectators to this debacle in his dining room.

"I said, get out," he seethed, pointing to the door.

"Not until we've got what we're looking for," Lawrence said, stepping farther into the room.

"And that would be?" Christopher blocked him with his body, refusing him any farther entrance.

"Ella Anston," said Lawrence, throwing a smug smile toward Ella. Christopher followed his gaze and saw Ella seemed to have shrunk in her seat as though she were trying to hide. "She stole from us, and we tracked her here. She comes with us, and we will leave the rest of you alone."

"Never!" said Anne, rising and standing between the two of them and Ella, as though she could shield her friend from them.

"Anne, don't," said Christopher and Ella at the same time, for once they agreed on something.

She looked at them both in turn. "Do *not* tell me what to do." Christopher flinched as if he'd been struck. Had she really just spoken to him like that, in front of polite company?

"You!" Anne cried, her focus now fixated on Kitty and Lawrence, her finger pointed toward them as she advanced on them, circling the table. "Who do you think you are, barging into Lord Merryweather's home, coming after Ella? She didn't steal from you, Lawrence, she took only what she was owed, as you decided not to pay her when she wouldn't perform particular favors for you."

Christopher heard someone gasp at that.

"And you, Kitty whatever your name is — not that anyone would know, since you are not particularly famous beyond your own inflated sense of self, you have some audacity showing your face here."

"Well," Kitty drawled, a catlike smile coming over her rouged lips. "It's a mite bit prettier than yours is now, isn't it love? Shame what happened to you on stage." She gave an exaggerated sigh. "Such a terrible accident."

Christopher could see the fury rising within Anne, as her hands became fists at her side, her body going rigid with tension.

"It was no accident, as you well know," Anne hissed. "You rigged that hook to fall. I could have been killed! Have you no compassion whatsoever? No thought to the wellbeing of others? It is appalling! It is … why it is…"

Christopher finally decided this had gone on long enough, and he took a step back from the two actors so that he could put a hand on Anne's back. Despite his horror at the entire situation, she seemed to need someone to lean on at the moment.

"It is time for the two of you to leave," he said. "From what I have heard, Miss Anston owes you nothing. Be off with you now, and never, ever return, or the authorities will become involved."

"Ah, so you are the champion of our little miss … what was it you called yourself? Annabelle Fredericks?" Lawrence asked, a smug grin covering his face, Christopher's words having no effect on him. Most people were reasonably afraid of the power a member of the nobility might hold, but apparently, Lawrence and Kitty were either ignorant or far too assured of their own ability to evade the law.

"At the moment, I am a man — an earl — who is commanding you to leave his home *at once*."

Lawrence reached behind him then, and in a swift motion pulled a dagger from the back of his belt, brandishing it in front of Christopher's face.

"And how would you, *My Lord*, like a scar to match your

little lady here, hmm?" he asked with a snarl. "I'll make sure it's nice and pretty, to match the rest of your face."

Anne gave a little squeak of shock, and in one quick motion, Christopher put himself bodily between her and the actor as he grabbed Lawrence's arm and, with a twist of his wrist, forced him to release the knife on the floor. Within moments he was surrounded by other gentlemen, and Lawrence quickly surrendered when he realized he had no chance to do anything more.

Christopher leaned over him.

"What do you feel Miss Anston owes you?'

The sum Lawrence named was laughable by Christopher's accounts, but he knew it would have large consequences for a woman such as Ella, with no other means of income.

"Very well," he said, matter-of-factly but with a hard edge to his words. "I will pay you what she owes, but you must promise to never, ever return, nor to ever come into contact with Lady Anne or Miss Anston again, do you understand me?"

Lawrence nodded, a glint coming into his eye when he was told he would be getting what he felt he was owed. Christopher hated the fact he was paying him off, but it would be worth it to ensure that the man never bothered them again.

"Come then," he said.

"Dibney!" he called to his butler, who was standing outside the door, still somewhat visibly shaken, although he seemed to have pulled himself together. "Fetch the money, will you, and then meet us at the servant's entrance."

He refused to take these people through the front door of his home. The butler looked as though he wanted to say something, to argue at their payout, but he nodded and

BECAUSE THE EARL LOVED ME

retreated. The sum was small enough that Dibney would have the funds within his own house accounts.

Christopher began to usher the two out the door when Anne's voice cut through the air behind them. "Wait!"

Annoyed now, he turned to her. What else could she possibly want?

She didn't look at him, however, but narrowed in on Kitty, her eyes boring into her.

"Admit it," she bit out, "admit what you did."

"And why would I do that?" the woman asked, raising an eyebrow.

"If you do not, I shall ensure life is made hell for you," Anne said. "My brother is a duke and has contacts through all of England. You will never act again, your name will be tarnished, and you shall have to leave the country if you ever wish to grace a stage again."

There was little chance the Duke of Breckenridge could actually do such a thing, but Kitty seemed a bit unsure of whether or not to believe Anne. Her eyes darted back and forth across her face, reminding Christopher of a trapped rodent.

"Fine," she finally seethed through tight lips. "I did it. I fixed the rope so it was loose and gave it a tug while you were performing. I didn't know what would happen — whether it would rip your gown, scare you, or yes, even kill you. The truth is, I didn't really care. You had no business being on that stage, and now, you will never return to it again, for your face is too hideous to watch for even a moment. Are you happy now?"

The woman smiled so smugly that Christopher wanted to wipe it off her face, but he kept himself under control. Anne, he could see, was having a difficult time of it, as her lip trembled, whether in upset or fury, he wasn't entirely sure. He looked at

Lady Honoria, catching her eye and tilting his head toward Anne. She nodded in understanding and rose to help her out of the room, while Christopher waved his hand out the door.

"Out, now, both of you," he said, following behind them. "I never want to see the pair of you again, as long as I live."

CHAPTER 23

No sooner had Honoria settled her in one of the drawing rooms — the blue one this time, the colder one, which Anne didn't particularly like, was she being honest — then Ella burst into the room after them, slamming the doors behind her.

"Oh, Anne!" she said, rushing over to them, kneeling in front of Anne and taking her hands in her own. "I am so sorry. I never thought they would find me here! Lord Merryweather is going to be awfully upset. I will leave right away, I promise, and will never bother you again."

Anne's own worries fled as she focused on Ella. The woman had told Anne shortly after arriving of the situation, making her promise not to say anything to anyone — including Christopher. She had been ashamed that a man would try to take her body against her will, and as much as Anne tried to convince her that it was not her fault at all, that it was all Lawrence's doing, Ella was sure she could be blamed for it.

"Sit up, Ella," she said now, pulling her onto the chesterfield next to them. "It's over now. The pair of them will get away with it, damn it all, but there's nothing to be done, I suppose. At least we are both free of them now. A confession is what I wanted, and I will have to be satisfied with that."

"Yes, but Lord Merryweather paid—"

"The sum will not hurt him, I don't think at all," said Anne, trying to soothe her concerns. "Besides that, if it is any issue, I have my own allowance from my brother, and I will repay Lord Merryweather."

She didn't express the fears that were flickering through her heart — that it wasn't at all the payment Lord Merryweather would be concerned about, but rather the scandal that would come down upon him, and how he felt about the spectacle that had been created in front of witnesses.

"He cares for you, Anne," Honoria said softly from beside her, apparently reading her thoughts. "He'll understand, will he not?"

"I hope so," she said softly. "He did stand up for me, didn't he, Honoria? The way he handled the two of them was rather wonderful."

Her heart warmed as she remembered it, the fierce look that had come over him as he stared down the actors, had defended her, had handled the entire situation. He was Alexander the Great, come to life in front of her eyes. "Perhaps," she whispered slowly. "Perhaps he—"

There came a knock at the door before it began to slowly open.

"Pardon the interruption," came his baritone voice, the one that sent tingles down Anne's spine. "Lady Anne, may I speak with you a moment?"

And then he filled the doorway, and she wanted nothing more than to stand and run to him, to wrap her arms around him and feel his protection engulf her. She held herself back, however, at the look on his face. His eyes were narrowed, his face pinched, and her stomach seemed to knot itself together as she feared the very worst.

"Excuse me," she whispered to Honoria and to Ella, who looked as though she wanted to say something, but Anne held up a hand, knowing it would only make the entire situation worse. "I will talk to you soon."

She joined Christopher at the door. He said nothing but held out an arm to lead her down the corridor to his office.

* * *

"My God, Anne," Christopher said, taking a seat behind his desk, resting his face in his hands as he ran his fingers through his hair. She took a seat in the chair in front of the desk, reaching out to touch him, but when he jerked away, she felt as though she had been burned.

She bit her lip as she waited for Christopher to say something. She looked around the office, so sparse and cold. It could do with some new decorating, she thought, picturing the carpet and the landscapes she could add to brighten it up.

"I don't know how much more of this I can take," he muttered, and she leaned forward toward him, hoping she hadn't heard him correctly.

"Excuse me?"

"I don't know if this is all worth it anymore!" he said with conviction now, standing.

"What is that supposed to mean?" she asked, her despair fading, being replaced by anger at his pigheadedness.

"I mean," he said intently, pacing back and forth behind his desk, his hands in fists at his side, belying how hard he was trying to keep himself in control. "I don't know if this — if you — are worth it any longer. First Ella, then this idiot from the theatre, that woman who hurt you. None of this would have happened had you not joined up with that bunch in the first place."

"I realize that," she said, trying to keep her voice calm and steady, throwing herself into the role of a governess, perhaps, requiring patience to keep her charges contained. "That was a mistake, Christopher, which we have been over time and again. Yes, there were repercussions from it, and for that I am sorry, but I don't know how much longer I can continue to apologize for it."

And if he expected her to do so one more time, he would be sorely disappointed.

He stopped, turning to face her, his arms crossed over his chest.

"When did you know about the money Miss Anston took from the theatre company?"

"She was owed that!" Anne said, defending her friend, and Christopher held up a hand.

"I am not disputing her claim," he said with more control now. "Unfortunately, the likelihood of it happening is very real, and I do not doubt that what she says is true. That was not, however, what I asked. When did you know of it?"

"When she arrived," Anne admitted but felt the need to attempt to defend herself. "She asked me not to say anything. She was ashamed."

"Anne," he said, his voice now emotionless, which somehow seemed all the worse. "You brought her to my home, to a party with many guests — including a duke and duchess. When something of such magnitude could possibly affect me — affect both of us — you cannot keep it a secret. I was your betrothed."

Was. Anne didn't miss the tense, cold beginning to seep through her veins.

"I realize she asked you to keep it to yourself, but you

should have told her the importance of informing me. Had I known, I could have kept this from happening."

"And how would you have done that?"

"By contacting the appropriate authorities, ensuring they saw to the issue," he said. "Though now that this Kitty has confessed, I will be sure that she does not get away with it."

"You would do that for me?" Anne asked, hope filling her.

"I would do it for anyone," he said, deflating her. "For it would be the right thing to do. Tell me, Anne," he continued, coming around the desk to stand before her. "And tell me the truth of it. When Ella said you were going to begin a theatre company, what did she mean by that?"

Anne felt the blood seep out of her face, her fingertips going cold. She pressed them together. She knew how upset he would be about this, but she had thought that if she was able to tell him at the right time, under the right circumstances, he would understand. It was actually an excellent plan, she thought, one that would allow her to bridge both of her worlds.

"Ella and I decided to start our own theatre company, it's true," she said, trying not to allow his glower to affect her as she wished the typically charming Lord Merryweather would return. She stood to try to rally her strength. "I wanted to tell you myself, but the timing was never quite right, and then Ella... well. We thought that we could start locally, get a few actors, try it out in town. We could put on a few plays. We wouldn't even need to make money to start, just—"

"Please tell me you are joking," he said, his lips tight, his body stiff and unrelenting. Despite how close he stood to her, he seemed so far away.

"I wouldn't jest about something like this," she said, desperate for him to understand. "I would have waited until after we were married, of course, but—"

"You were going to do this as the Countess of Merryweather?"

"Well, who else would I be?"

"Anne Finchley, sister of the Duke of Breckenridge," he said, his face hard and unyielding. "When are you going to understand that my wife will not be parading around in costumes, putting on shows for any commoner to watch?"

"And when are you going to understand that I will never be the proper wife who behaves exactly as society believes she should? I love you, Christopher. That's right, I love you, as stubborn and inflexible as you may be. And I will be your wife in every way, free from scandal but for this one exception. I just ask that you love me for the person I truly am. If you cannot do that, then I …" her voice broke and fell to a whisper, "I do not know how else we can be happy together."

They stood facing one another, both breathing hard, the tension between them so terrifyingly taut, Anne began to feel the inside of her chest cracking as her heart broke, for as much as she loved him, she would never let him crush her spirit, to turn her into someone she could never be. She waited for him to say something, to tell her he loved her for the person she was.

He opened his mouth, but closed it again, looking down at the plain cream rug on the floor as he brought his hands to his hips, then set them back down again.

"I—" he began, and then rubbed at his forehead. "I care for you, Anne, I do, but — this behavior has to stop."

"Very well," she finally said after choking down a sob, as she now knew he would never say the words she longed to hear. A haunted look covered his face. "I think we both know what has to happen now. Goodbye, Christopher."

CHAPTER 24

Two months later
London, England

ANNE PUT her feet up on the arm of the chesterfield, holding her book up above her face. It was bloody dreary, and it didn't take long for her to throw it to the floor dramatically. She stared at the gilded light fixture above her, its glass seeming to rain down on her, for a moment before getting up and pacing to the window, looking down on the Mayfair street below. Nothing to see of any note. She sighed, and walked to the canvas in the corner, looking down on the blank piece of paper staring back at her, waiting for color and life to fill it, but she had nothing inside of her to give to it.

Finally, she made her way to the pianoforte. This was essentially her drawing room for the season, as Olivia would likely remain in the country. Her mother was here with her, of course, determined that Anne would now make a match. Her mother, however, was overly optimistic, thought Anne.

She had told Lady Cecelia that she wasn't likely to make a match anymore, that no one would want her. She not only now had a scandal attached to her name and a scar covering her face, but she had been rejected by one of the most eligible bachelors in all of England.

Anne's elbows dropped onto the keys, causing a disastrous chord to sound through the room. She placed her head in her hands. Ella had fled from Christopher's estate two months ago, ashamed by all that had happened, and Anne hadn't seen her since. The season had yet to fully begin, and since her return to London, Anne hadn't received any callers, which was in such contrast to the parade of young men and women who had before frequented their home. It seemed, apparently, that no one wanted anything more to do with her.

"I say, I have never heard such a melancholy chord!"

"Honoria!" Anne jumped from the bench, ran to her friend, and threw her arms around her. "Oh, you are the first bit of happiness I have had in days and days. How fortunate I am to have a friend who still believes in me."

Honoria laughed and returned Anne's embrace.

"You could cause a scandal with the Prince Regent himself, Anne, and I wouldn't leave you," she said. "That is not what it means to be a friend."

"If only most felt that way," she said with a sigh, releasing Honoria and leading her to the small sitting area, where she resumed her previous seat on the chesterfield while Honoria took the sofa across from her.

"You are speaking of Lord Merryweather, I suppose?" Honoria asked.

"I suppose I am," Anne said with a shrug. "Though what does it matter anymore? He has no care for me, and apparently he never really did."

"I do not think that is true," Honoria said gently. "He may

come around yet, you never know. Perhaps he will realize how impulsively he acted."

"He never acts on impulse. And if he did, he would never admit it," said Anne morosely, fisting her gown between her fingers.

"Well," said Honoria, leaning toward her. "You are not a woman who is meant to sit and despair of her life. Why do we not go to the theatre tonight? That always cheers you up some."

"I don't think so," said Anne, shaking her head. "That will only remind me of everything that has brought about my downfall."

"Anne," said Honoria gently, her head tilted to the side. "Your first love has always been the theatre. Do not let it be taken away from you. That would be the greatest tragedy of all."

"What is playing?" Anne asked, trying not to let her interest show, though it had been some time since she had seen anything.

"The Way of the World."

"Oh," said Anne softly, "I do love that play."

"Very well, it is settled," said Honoria. "My cousin and I shall attend with you and your mother, how is that?"

Anne shrugged. "I suppose, but only with you, Honoria."

Honoria nodded, standing to depart. "Now, Anne, no more of this self-pity. I would like my friend back. Begin your return tonight."

* * *

"Lord Merryweather, how wonderful to see you!"

He turned to the voice, seeing all three Winterton girls approaching at a rapid pace. He wasn't sure which one of them had spoken — did it really matter? In his blurred gaze they all looked very similar, in their creamy white dresses, their dark hair piled high on their heads in ringlets. He preferred blonde hair. Sandy-blonde hair. Especially down around the shoulders — her shoulders. He stumbled a bit.

"Get a hold of yourself, man," came a voice in his ear. Oh yes. Watson. He had come with Watson. Actually, Watson was the reason he had come at all. Damn the man. He didn't want to be here. He didn't want to be speaking with Winterton Girl One, Two, or Three. He wanted to be home in his library, a glass of brandy in his hand.

"Lady Winterton has said hello to you," Watson said, and Christopher grunted when he felt the man poke him in the side. "Respond, then we will be off to private quarters. You are not fit for company."

"Good to see you again," he said with what he hoped was a friendly wave, and Watson said something that Christopher didn't quite hear before he found himself pushed forward.

"What was that for?" he grunted.

"You are quite sauced, and you are making a fool of yourself," Watson said. "You just about smacked Lady Winterton in the face. I should never have brought you here."

"On that, we can agree," Christopher said.

He wasn't really sure what was playing that evening. He had never much liked the theatre, but now he detested it passionately. Watson, however, had refused to take no for an answer when it came to tonight's entertainment.

""Look, Merryweather, You've never been one to enjoy drink," Watson said once they had found their box. "I know you feel you have been wronged, but if you miss Lady Anne so much, why not resume her acquaintance?"

Christopher shook his head. He was done with her and she with him. So he missed her — desperately. He wasn't about to tell Watson that. Besides, he had found a new friend in his drink. It warmed him and it kept him company. He had been missing out for so long.

"In fact," Watson continued. "I believe she is here tonight. Look across from us, two boxes below."

Christopher didn't want to look. He wasn't going to. But suddenly he was compelled to follow where Watson's finger pointed. It didn't take long at all to find her. The blonde of her hair, the blue of her dress — her favorite color, he knew. She looked … well, she looked like hell, he thought, noting the paleness of her face without her usual rosy cheeks, her hair limp around her head, her face pinched. The thought should have made him feel some sort of satisfaction, but instead, it simply filled him with an even deeper melancholy than before. He had never wanted her to feel such sorrow. He didn't want to see her hurt. And now, she was not only clearly suffering, but it was his own fault.

He rose from his seat.

"I'm going home, Watson," he said, grabbing onto the rail for balance. "You can come with me — or not."

* * *

"Isn't this wonderful tonight?" Honoria asked, but Anne found she could offer no exuberance to match Honoria's excitement. She simply shrugged her shoulders. "I suppose."

"Of course it is, Lady Honoria," Anne's mother said from her other side, likely trying to make up for Anne's lack of excitement. "Thank you so much for having us."

Anne had insisted they not stop to talk to anyone but make their way straight to the box. She had taken the first step by coming here tonight. To actually speak with others in society would have to wait for another night, a night when she had more courage.

"Oh, Anne," Honoria said with some compassion. "Forget

Lord Merryweather. Forget the gossips. Simply think of the wonderment that is on stage!"

That was the problem. Every time Anne looked at the stage, all she could think of was her own failure, her own accident, the injury that had forever put a stop to all that she had envisioned in her life. For a time she had hoped she could still have all that she had longed for, but she knew now that she was being foolish. As always.

Sudden movement across the theatre caught her eye, and she saw a man stand. *That is rather rude*. With a jolt, she realized the man now making his way out of the box, slightly stumbling, was none other than Christopher. It had been so long since she had seen him, though his face seemed to be permanently imprinted on her mind. He stopped for a moment, as if he could feel her gaze upon him. He searched the seats across from him, and then his eyes locked on hers. He was close enough that she could see his strong, lean frame had thinned out somewhat, his typically immaculate attire was askew, and he seemed to wobble a bit as he stood. His eyes narrowed and he ripped his gaze away from her, continuing to move toward the exit.

Anne felt a storm begin to build in her chest at his rejection.

"I want to go home, Honoria," she said, horror filling her as her eyes began to water. "I am done with this."

She was done with everything. With the stage, with society, and most especially, with love.

CHAPTER 25

Well, at least she had thought she was done with it all. Until her mother had begged — begged! — her to attend the season's first ball. Not the official season, not quite yet, but the first where all who wanted to be seen would be in attendance.

"Oh, Anne, it will not be so terrible," her mother had said that morning once she rose. "I'm sure everyone will have completely forgotten by now what happened to you."

"I hardly think that will be the case," Anne said, throwing back her hands, accompanied by a dramatic eye roll. "The season has just begun, and there are far fewer scandals throughout the summer, you know that, Mother. I will be the evening's entertainment."

"There is only one way to get past it," her mother said. "Keep your chin up, put on a brave face, and show them that no one can get to you. Besides, what else are you going to do? Sit here in the townhouse all season? I hardly think so." She lifted a hand to Anne's cheek. "Don't forget how much you love the dancing and the gowns and the flirtations.

Remember how all would watch every time you graced the floor!" Her face took on a dreamy expression.

"Things change, Mother," Anne said morosely.

"Then change them back," her mother said with more surprising determination. "You must come, Anne. I have not seen anyone for ages, and it would very odd if you did not accompany me."

So, feeling guilty for leaving her mother alone, here Anne was, sitting among the wallflowers — ladies she had never dreamed she would become a part of — hoping she would become one with the floral wallpaper behind her. She kept her head down, staring at her hands in her lap. *Just a few hours. Get through this and go home. A couple of weeks and a new scandal will emerge and all will forget you. Or by then you can propose a plan to run away, to begin life anew. Yes. That's it. No more of this. No more pretension. No—*

"Well, if it isn't Lady Anne Finchley."

Good Lord, no. Anyone but her. Anyone.

Anne took a deep breath and swallowed hard. She wanted to run as far from here as she could, but she vowed she would never give Gertrude the satisfaction. She rose to her feet, remembering her mother's words and holding her chin as high as she could.

"Lady Rumsfelter," she said, forcing a smile to her lips, "how lovely to see you."

"And you," Gertrude said, the glint in her eyes telling. "I never expected to see you here this evening — or this season at all, really. Oh, I love what you've done with your hair. Your maid has done very well in … attempting … to hide your scar with those ringlets."

Anne clenched her fists but maintained her smile. That had been exactly what Bridget had been trying to do, but she wasn't going to admit as much to Gertrude.

"Now, Anne, you *must* tell me about Lord Merryweather,"

Gertrude said. "When I last saw you, he claimed to be your betrothed, but now I have heard that perhaps that is no longer the case."

Anne wanted to deny what she said, simply because she hated the smirk of satisfaction that covered Gertrude's face, but she wasn't going to hide behind a lie.

"We are not betrothed," she said, forcing the words out. "As I am sure you well know, Gertrude."

"Oh my," Gertrude breathed, "whatever happened?"

"I would prefer not to speak of it at the moment," Anne said, as a lump began to form in her throat and tears burned the backs of her eyes.

"Oh, you poor darling," Gertrude said with faint mockery. "Well," she leaned in, "what I witnessed earlier now makes sense. I saw Lord Merryweather at the beginning of the evening. He and one of the Ladies Winterton looked quite enamored with one another, and I thought to myself, surely he wouldn't be carrying on so while betrothed to poor Anne!" She tittered. "I am so glad that was not the case. Well, then Lady Anne, I wish you all the best in securing a suitor this season. If anyone can overcome all of the odds against her, I am sure it would be you."

She turned then, joining a group of women a short distance away, and it wasn't long before they were all looking Anne's way and laughing. Anne tried to maintain her dignity. She tried to stare back at them without betraying herself and showing them just how much their words hurt. But it all became more than she could bear, and she turned around, suddenly desperate to find refuge. She was not fleeing. She was simply finding a moment alone.

* * *

CHRISTOPHER HAD MANAGED to restrain himself to two drinks tonight. Watson had told him in no uncertain terms that any more than that and he would no longer be speaking to him. He sighed as he surveyed the room. He didn't want to be here, with all of the vapid society ladies, the pretentious lot of the *ton*, so eager to bring down one another. And yet, here he was, trying to distract himself from thoughts of *her*.

When he had seen Anne last night, he finally admitted to himself what he had known deep inside since the moment she had left his home. He had made a huge mistake. His house had become as empty and lonely as his heart. He hadn't realized, when he turned Anne away, how much she had filled a hole in his life, in his soul, that he never knew had been there. But now that she was gone, what was left behind was a sense of despair, one that he didn't know how to be rid of.

He leaned back against the wall, surveying the room. The Ladies Winterton were here — of course. Their mother was pushing them at every titled gentleman that walked by. They had set upon him once he entered, but after he responded with a few polite but short words, they had given up and left him alone. Now one of them was attempting to charm Watson beside him, who could barely get a word in, the woman was blabbering on so much.

Christopher continued to look around the room. For whom, he wasn't sure. Certainly Anne wouldn't be here. She had barely been able to remain at the theatre the previous night — Watson told him that she had left at intermission. She was still on the tongues of many gossips. They both were — that much was apparent by the many looks that had been sent his way throughout the evening. It would be much, much worse, for her, he knew. He was simply a note in the story. She *was* the story.

His eyes stopped, alighting on a conversation in the

corner. And then his heart stopped as well. For there she was. Anne. His Anne. Oh, why had he been such a fool? She was back against the wall, a place he had never seen her before, a place she didn't belong. She was talking to someone, whom, he wasn't sure, but the look on her face became rather desperate. Christopher began pushing his way through the crowd, his need to get to her overcoming all else. If only he could speak to her. He had been proud, too proud, too foolish, but perhaps he could finally make things right.

He came up behind the pair as he heard Lady Rumsfelter's last words, discussing his own conversation with a Lady Winterton. The lies this woman told! Anger curled within him, and as she turned away, Christopher began to follow her to ask — politely — that she not spread such falsehoods about him, but then he saw the look on Anne's face. She hadn't seen him yet. Instead, she was staring across the room, following Lady Rumsfelter, watching her return to her friends, witnessing their laughter. Then, with all the regality of a queen, she turned and began to stride from the room. Christopher paused for a moment before following her, but the moment she was out of the ballroom, she broke into a run, hurrying down the corridor, before she apparently found a suitable room and escaped into it, slamming the door shut behind her.

"Anne!" Christopher called, knocking on the door. "May I come in?"

Hearing nothing, he turned the doorknob, easing the door open, finding himself in a small library, though Anne was nowhere to be seen.

"Anne?" he called again, and he began to search down one row of books after another until he finally found her in between shelves in the back corner. There were tears rolling down her face, and Christopher's heart broke. This should never have happened. She never should be feeling such pain.

"Anne," he said once more, reaching out to her, wanting to comfort her from all she was going through.

"Don't touch me!" she cried, shrinking away from him, and he dropped his arms to his side.

"Anne, I am so sorry," he said desperately, hoping she could understand how truly contrite he was. "I never meant to hurt you. I was wrong. I let my pride, my ... arrogance, if you will, come between us. I am sorry Anne, I truly am. Will you give me another chance?"

She looked up at him then, hurt swimming in her eyes.

"Christopher..." she whispered, astonishment overcoming her face. "You haven't spoken to me, not a word, for two months, since the day I confessed my love to you and you turned me away. You utterly broke my heart, making me look even more foolish than I already did, and now you believe that with a simple apology I will fall back into your arms?"

Well, yes actually, that was what he had been thinking, though it would not be particularly clever to tell her such. He hadn't had much time to formulate a plan, as all seemed to have changed the moment he saw her.

"You hurt me, Christopher, worse than I could ever have imagined," she continued. "I know you did much for me. You came after me when I needed rescue. You didn't judge me — not at first — but allowed me to heal, to overcome my pain. You stayed with me when I needed a friend, despite how I was taking you away from your life, from your plans. And you agreed to marry me in order to save me from humiliation."

Hope began to fill him. If she recognized all of this, did that mean she might forgive him?

"But then," she continued with a sigh, and his heart sank, "you turned away from me when it all became too much for your plan for your perfect life. You rejected me, Christopher.

And the thing is, life isn't perfect. Life isn't controllable. And if it was, then where would the fun be? I know you need your plans, your predictability. I understand that, and I was more than willing to follow along, to do what you needed, to be there for you as long as there was room for some give and take. But you left no such opening, Christopher."

"I realize that now," he said, hearing the despair in his voice. "It took me far too long to come to understand it, I know that, Anne. I was a fool. These last two months have been hell. I have longed to come to you, to tell you how I felt, but I was simply too proud. It is another addition to the list of what I must be forgiven for."

She sighed, looking down at the floor.

"Unfortunately, Christopher, that is one list that will not be checked off," she said, shaking her head with regret, her voice slightly breaking. "You need a wife who will remain proper and poised, whose name will never grace the scandal sheets. A woman who will be perfectly happy with simply being your countess and looking after your home. While I would love you more than any and could do a fine job of running your estate, I need more than that in my life, and you cannot accept that. Therefore, we can never be."

"But I love you, Anne," he said desperately. This was not how he wanted to tell her, but all of the light and laughter she brought to his life was worth more than anything he could have ever imagined. "I do."

"It's too late," she said sadly, then, taking him completely off guard, she brushed past him toward the door. "Goodbye, Christopher."

CHAPTER 26

"Anne?"

"Alastair!"

If there was one thing that could cheer her up, it was her brother. Anne rose from her seat at the dinner table, hurrying to greet him at the dining room door. She nearly cried when his arms came around her, in a rare show of affection. Somehow, he must have known she needed the comfort tonight.

It had been a week since she had last seen Christopher, and she had hoped that finally having the opportunity to tell him all she felt would give her closure and allow her to move on. But seeing him, how broken he was, hearing his words, only made her feel even more wretched. When he had told her he loved her, she had wanted so badly to agree to whatever he wanted of her, if it meant that she could be with him again. But she knew, deep in her heart, that to give up on her greatest passion would only lead to a future of regret and resentment.

"How fares Hannah? Olivia?"

Alastair took a seat next to her at the table and began to

answer all her questions, telling her all she wanted to hear, the news she craved. Their mother had already left for the evening to attend a function, but this time Anne had refused to go along. It was, in fact, why Alastair was here — Anne was determined to return to the country for some time while she decided what she would do with her life, where she would go from here.

"When would you like to leave?" she asked him, once they had discussed the matter.

"Soon," he said "tomorrow, actually. I don't want to leave Olivia for long."

"I understand," she said, eager to leave London behind. "I will have my maid ensure all is prepared."

Their mother had been despondent that Alastair remained for such a short while, but once they began their journey, Anne felt a sense of relief come over her — so much so, that she was able to lay her head back against the squabs and finally relax. The carriage's rocking motion was oddly soothing, and soon she nodded off into a blessedly contented sleep.

* * *

SHE WOKE to stillness and sat up when she felt the cool air blowing through the carriage door. She looked around to find that Alastair had already disembarked.

"Alastair?" she called, poking her head out the door and beginning to descend down the steps. "Where are we? This is not…."

This was not her home, no. This was Gracebourne — Christopher's home.

She turned to find Alastair standing behind her, blocking her escape back to the carriage. Her heart began to quicken as the sight of his house brought panic to her breast. She didn't want to face this — not again.

"Alastair, what is the meaning of this? Let me back in that carriage right *now*!"

"Anne," he said calmly, unaffected by her dramatics as he held up a hand. "We can go, but there is something you need to see first."

"Alastair, Christopher and I ... we do not suit one another. Time and again, we have proven to be too different, unable to find a way to be together without one of us losing ourselves. You know, this — or do I need to go over the entire sordid story again?"

"I do understand, Anne," he responded, with a look of chagrin. "And yet, despite all that has happened I also know he loves you, very much. He came to see me and he is devastated. He needs you."

"I am not so sure about that," she said, hearing the bite to her tone as she no longer wanted to speak of this with her brother. "And I do not need *him*!"

"Are you sure about that?" he asked gently. "Come. Give him one hour. If at that time, you still wish to go, we will be on our way. Can you do that? I won't force you Anne, but please, I beg you, just an hour."

She sighed, turning to see Christopher waiting at the entrance to his home, his hands clasped behind his back as he paced back and forth before the stately door.

"Fine," she said, turning back to Alastair, "one hour. That's it."

They walked up the long drive, Alastair's hand behind her back, and she appreciated the support, as angry as she was over being duped.

"If I hadn't been asleep," she murmured, "would you have told me where we were going?"

"No," he said, and she heard the laughter in his voice, "for you would have likely jumped from the carriage."

She nearly laughed then, but they had come close enough that she could see Christopher's face. He looked … haunted. Yet hopeful at the same time.

Oh, how she longed to run up and throw her arms around him, to tell him how wonderful it was to see him, that she was sorry she had rejected him. But she quelled herself. *He is not the man for you, Anne. The two of you cannot be together and satisfied with your lives.* She tried to fix a sweet smile on her face, one that would not reveal what she truly felt. He was a friend — an acquaintance — she was pleased to see. That was all. *Liar.*

"Anne," he said, his face masked as she and Alastair walked up to the door. Belatedly he nodded to her brother. "Breckenridge, thank you."

Anne gave her brother a look out of the corner of her eye. She knew he wanted her married to Christopher — or simply married, most likely — but this was quite beyond anything she would have thought him capable of. It was not as though *his* marriage had been particularly conventional. Had anyone tried to force him to wed, he would have run the other way. He only married because he had given *himself* no other choice. Oh, he would hear exactly what she thought on the carriage ride home. For now, though, she and Christopher apparently had something to discuss.

He held out his arm to her.

"Will you accompany me for a moment? There is something I would like to show you."

"Very well," she said with a nod, keeping her gaze in front of her as he led her through the foyer and down the corridor toward the back of the house. She knew there were primarily unused rooms here. A conservatory that he had kept tidy, but barren. A drawing room or two with the furniture covered in cloth. She had explored Gracebourne when she was here previously — she had been unable to help her curiosity.

He pushed open the door to the conservatory, beckoning her to enter ahead of him. She walked in, unsure of what to expect, and came to a sudden stop as shock washed over her.

"Christopher?" she whispered, her hand coming to her mouth.

For standing in front of her was the most glorious stage she had ever seen in her life. Gone were the plants which were barely surviving and the useless old furniture that had been shoved into the forgotten room. Sun shone through the tall windows onto the wooden platform, which apparently had been recently built as the entire room smelled of fresh-hewn timber. Lush, velvet red curtains were suspended from the ceiling, and in front of the stage were rows of chairs for an audience. There still were a few plants around the outskirts of the room, and it seemed they were actually being cared for.

"What is this?" she asked, breathless, but Christopher said nothing. He simply smiled at her nervously then walked to the stage, up the steps and to the center of it. Anne was drawn toward him, as he stood looking very uncomfortable. He cleared his throat and rolled his shoulders.

He took a deep breath.

"Let me not to the marriage of true minds
Admit impediments. Love is not love
Which alters when it alteration finds,
Or bends with the remover to remove:
O no! It is an ever-fixed mark
That looks on tempests and is never shaken;
It is the star to every wandering bark,
Whose worth's unknown, although his height be taken.
Love's not Time's fool, though rosy lips and cheeks
Within his bending sickle's compass come:

Love alters not with his brief hours and weeks,
But bears it out even to the edge of doom.
If this be error and upon me proved,
I never writ, nor no man ever loved."

As he finished the words, he began walking off the stage toward her, where she stood transfixed. For once in her life, Anne had no idea what to say, how to respond, or what to even think.

Christopher bent down on one knee in front of her, took her hands in his, and slipped her gloves off. Her skin seemed to burn where he touched her, and she thought if her heart beat any faster, she was likely to fall over in a faint.

"Shakespeare's Sonnet 116," she finally whispered, to which he nodded.

"Anne," he said, his voice thick with emotion, "I know words only mean so much, I do. But I do not know how else to tell you how much I truly love you. I was wrong before. I was more of a fool than I could ever have thought possible. I thought you didn't fit in my life, but I could not have been more mistaken. For you fill every hole in my home, in my soul, in my heart. Everything that I am lacking, you fill with your love, your laughter, your light. This stage is yours, whether you choose me or not. You can put on plays, invite actors, direct the villagers — whatever you choose. I only want you to be happy. If you choose to travel to act elsewhere, I only ask that when you come home, come home to me."

At his words, Anne did as she had been longing to do, and launched herself into his arms, with so much force that he went sprawling backward with her on top of him. She took his face in her hands and kissed him then, long and hard, hungry for him and all that he had promised her. She had been wrong. She had thought that they clashed too violently to find a life together, but, in fact, he was right — in all actuality, their strengths and weaknesses complemented one another. They simply had to each put aside their own stubbornness to understand that.

Finally, he gently pushed her slightly away from him so that his eyes could search hers.

"Is that a yes?"

"Oh, yes, Christopher, yes a thousand times over! I do love you, so much. And I don't want to travel, but I do want to act, I want to sing. I can hardly believe you did this for me — it is the most romantic thing I have ever seen in my entire life, whether on stage or in a book or in the true world. And when I am not acting, I promise I shall be perfectly proper."

She started crying then, unstoppable tears running down her face, and Christopher sat up, resting her on his lap.

"What is this? Is everything all right?"

"It's more than all right," she said with a hiccup, sobbing now. "This is the last of the dramatics, I promise!"

He started laughing then, a chuckle that echoed around the room.

"I love you, Anne Finchley, with all that I am."

"And I love you, Christopher Anderson, and will for the rest of my life."

CHAPTER 27

It was fortunate that Breckenridge had retained the special license. For once Christopher and Anne decided they were going to be married, no one wanted to wait any longer. Not Anne, not Breckenridge — he was too nervous they would call it off again — and certainly not Christopher.

Anne and her brother had stayed the day before returning home. Breckenridge had given them time alone — although he was quick to remind them, several times in fact, that he was not too terribly far away, and Christopher spent the time giving Anne a very thorough tour of his home. There were so many rooms that hadn't been opened in years, save for the servants giving them a quick dust now and again. Anne's eyes gleamed, and Christopher knew she was beginning to think of all she could do with them, and — hopefully — the children they would have to fill the rooms and the large, dreary halls. His heart glowed with the fact that she had taken to her role of countess with gusto. His servants were enamored with her exuberance, though she had been careful to ensure that he was agreeable to any suggested changes.

"You have been here but a day, and already this house feels like much more of a home," he said, grinning at her as they sat on a bench in his gardens outside of the conservatory — or what Anne now referred to as "the glorious theatre."

"Oh, don't be silly, Christopher," she said. "You've lived your whole life here."

"True," he nodded, "but since my mother died and my sister married, it has been so quiet. When my mother was alive, this house was filled with light and laughter. But since then ... well, my father became unreachable after that." He sobered, "I have always been far too concerned with acting in the right way by trying to do what is proper, what is expected. But you have made me realize that what is right is not always what others believe, but what your heart tells you."

He smiled at her animated face, now stretched into a wide smile. She leaned her head against his shoulder, snuggling in close.

"And what does your heart tell you now, Christopher?"

"That life without you is no life at all."

She leaned up then and kissed him softly, and her lips on his were the sweetest thing he had ever before felt. His arms came around her and he pulled her in close, complete in the knowledge that she would be his for the rest of his life. He sighed and smiled. He had no desire to work at checking off a list, nor making any further plans — at the moment, at least. For now, he would simply sit and enjoy this time with her.

*　*　*

One week later

. . .

CHRISTOPHER CLIMBED the freshly hewn stairs — only the second time he had done so — and looked out at the small number of people who had gathered in the rows of chairs in front of him. It was the first performance to be put on this stage in front of a true audience, and he could think of nothing that would be more enjoyable.

Breckenridge had wanted the wedding to be at his home, but Anne had insisted she be married here, on the stage of her new theatre. He had finally agreed when Olivia had promised that she and the baby would be well enough to make the trip, despite the physician's orders otherwise.

"I can't take one more minute shut up in this house!" she had said and didn't see any issue in the two of them leaving for one night, along with the nurse.

The crowd — Anne's family and a few friends, including Watson, Lady Honoria, and even Ella — stirred as they heard something at the back of the room, and the conservatory doors opened to reveal Christopher's bride. His breath caught as he looked at her on the arm of her brother. She wore a long, pale pink dress, highlighted with beautiful beading and embroidery up and down the sides. Her hair was piled high on her head but flowed down in gentle waves about her face. Her smile was radiant, and how much better it felt to be the cause of her joy rather than her tears. Never again would he hurt her as he had done, he vowed, nor allow anyone else to do so either.

She climbed the stage's side stairs, and Christopher shook Breckenridge's hand before the Duke returned to his seat below. Anne came to him, grasped his hands, and gave him a quick kiss, causing laughter among their witnesses. The vicar cleared his throat and frowned, but Anne just smiled at him and held up a finger.

"Before we start, I just have one thing I want to say," she

said, and the vicar looked perturbed, but she was the sister of a powerful duke, marrying the lord who oversaw the village of his parsonage, and so he motioned for her to continue.

"Christopher," she said, turning to him as she took a small piece of paper from her gown's bodice. Christopher grinned widely and tried not to laugh as the vicar began to sputter. She turned and frowned at the man, but continued her lines.

"I want you to know how much I appreciate the fact that you accept me for who I am, and for what my passions are. I also want *you* to know that I love you for you, and while I appreciate the fact that we will compromise, I don't want you to change. So I have made a list of what I love about you, and why."

She cleared her throat, and looked down at her paper and read.

"First, I love your lists. I think they are very practical, and, in fact, they ensure that things are completed in a timely fashion. This is something that I am not particularly adept at, and therefore it is fortunate that my husband is.

"Second, I love that you make plans. For it means that you care, that you put time and effort into seeing after the affairs of others, and that nothing and no one is left unaccounted for.

"Third, I love that you put the concerns of others before yourself. You left your entire life behind to come find me when I needed you, despite your *very* obvious disapproval.

"Fourth, I love the fact that you are too stubborn to realize you have the worst sense of direction of anyone I have ever met. For, if you did not have this flaw, you would be altogether too perfect, and I would feel incredibly stupid beside you.

"I could go on and on, but I will tell you the rest later as I'm sure everyone is growing rather bored. But fifth, I love how much you love me and how much I know you will love whatever family we have to come."

Christopher looked down at his hands as his eyes begin to burn, and he blinked rapidly to keep any moisture away. He took her hands and kissed the knuckles of each finger.

"I don't deserve you," he whispered.

"Of course you do," she said with a look of consternation. "Were you not listening to me? I just told you all of the reasons why!"

The vicar took a step forward, nearly forcing them away from one another.

"This is all very untoward," he said, and while Christopher agreed, he didn't much care at the moment. "Can we get on with it?"

"We can," they said in unison, and the vicar motioned for them to drop their hands and face him, and then quickly began to cite the marriage vows before he was interrupted again.

Anne was very subdued through the remainder of the ceremony, saying her lines as she was supposed to, although when the vicar asked, "Do you promise to love and obey...." she cocked an eyebrow at the words, and when she twisted her lips, Christopher knew she was trying not to smile.

"I — I do."

"Very good," the vicar said before continuing, and Christopher knew that he would spend the rest of his life wondering what would next come out of her mouth. It would be an adventure, that much was certain.

When the ceremony was over, when they had left the theatre and stood on the other side of the doors, Christopher finally planted a firm kiss on her lips before the rest of their company came out to join them.

They weren't quick enough, as he heard Breckenridge

clearing his throat. He looked as though he were about say something, but then he threw up his hands and grinned. "Never mind," he said, "she's yours to deal with now."

Anne swatted her brother's arm before he gave her a warm embrace, and soon enough they all went off to celebrate with a wedding breakfast. All had been thrown together so quickly it wasn't the most elaborate meal, but they seemed to enjoy it anyway.

There was one person, however, who Christopher had to speak to before this celebration was complete. After breakfast, they had all retired to the drawing room. Typically, the gentlemen would stay in the dining room for some time to celebrate on their own, but Christopher had decided that this day was meant to be spent with his bride.

"Miss Anston?" he said, as the tall, dark-haired woman began to walk by him, having given him only the smallest of smiles and a simple "congratulations."

"Do you have a moment? There is something I should like to discuss with you."

"Of course," she said, though she didn't seem too incredibly enthused about it — not that Christopher blamed her. He drew her over to the side of the room, beside a window looking out over the grounds. Christopher noted her gaze was on the gardens beneath them, as she avoided looking directly at him.

"Miss Anston, I haven't been fair to you," he said, and her head swiveled toward him, shock in her eyes. Somehow these apologies were getting easier the more he made them. "I blamed you for much of what Anne went through, but in reality, it was not your fault at all. You were simply a reminder of what had happened, and it was painful for me to recall it. I was rude to you when you did nothing but help Anne at the time she needed it the most. Do you forgive me for it?"

She stared at him for a moment, as though she was unsure of what to say, of how to respond to him. "I — of course," she said finally.

Relief flowed through Christopher. Who would have thought that keeping from his stubborn ways would actually lift some of the burdens off of him?

"I understand, My Lord," she said. "It must have been difficult to see someone you love injured like that."

"You do not need to use 'my lord' with me, Miss Anston, for you are a friend of the family."

Her face lit up in a warm smile.

"Since you left here, where have you been living?" He knew Anne had found her after a thorough search, an investigation she relished, but he didn't know the full details.

"In the village, actually," she said, looking down to the ground. "The physician does not live close, and it seems help is needed in treating common ailments and the like. I didn't want to go back to the theatre. It was not just that company. I never really loved acting. I was good at it, though, and I made decent money. I had really just been running away, however. But I've found — I like it here."

"Do you have a place to live?"

"I do," she said. "A lovely couple has taken me in. Their children are grown and gone, and it seems to be as good a place as any for a time."

"You always have a room here, if you'd like."

"Thank you My Lo— Lord Merryweather, I do appreciate that," she said. "But I think I would like to make my own way for a while."

"Very well," he replied, "do not be a stranger, Miss Anston."

"Rest assured she will not!" said Anne, joining them, a smile wreathing her face, as she was apparently pleased to see the two of them getting on so well.

"Of course not," Ella replied. "I wish you nothing but happiness. I best get going. Farewell, Anne, Lord Merryweather."

"Goodbye, Ella."

CHAPTER 28

Anne loved entertaining, but she was actually relieved when the rest of her guests left that afternoon. She had wanted to get Christopher alone for some time, and now that they were married, well, there was nothing holding her back any longer.

She went to find him when the butler and the housekeeper stopped her.

"May we speak with you, My Lady?"

"Of course," she said, looking from one of them to the other, "is something amiss?"

"Oh, not at all!" the housekeeper, Mrs. Allen, replied.

"In fact, rather the opposite," added the butler.

"We just wanted to say, how happy we are to have you here, My Lady. Lord Merryweather has never been so … content," said Mrs. Allen.

"Ah, and he has left you alone, finally, is that it?" Anne said, raising her eyebrows.

"Oh, we meant nothing of the sort, My Lady," said Dibney quickly. "We simply meant—"

"It's quite all right," she said, patting his arm as she smiled at Mrs. Allen. "I completely understand. Lord Merryweather has a tendency to get slightly too … involved in all matters that concern him."

"We simply don't want him to worry over things he has no need to," said Mrs. Allen.

"Understood," Anne replied, "I will be sure to keep him busy."

As she walked away, a smile, one the servants couldn't see, came over her face as she thought of just how she would entertain him. Now, she just had to find him, and she would begin her task.

"Christopher?" she called, finally discovering him in his office. "Our guests have just departed. What in the heavens are you doing?"

"I had something simple to look over, just to reassure myself," he said, his gaze on his papers. "I will be but a moment, and then once it is off my mind, I am yours for the rest of the day, I promise."

He scratched a few things on the paper in front of him — likely a list, Anne thought with some mirth, before he raised his head and found her once more.

"There — finished," he said, putting his pen back in the groove on his desk, tidying his papers into an even stack and then coming around to her, drawing her in close.

"Now, wife, is there something on your mind?"

She looked up at him coyly and smiled.

"Yes, but I think I am going to have to show you."

"Show me? Where?"

"Follow me."

Her heart beat fast as she took his hand and led him out of the office, down the corridor and around the bend until they reached what she knew to be his bedroom.

"Christopher," she said, stopping in front of his door. "I

know it is all well and proper that we have separate bedrooms. I, however, disagree."

"Do you?"

"I do. I know you may not want the same, but I am going to make a strong argument for why we should share the same room — and the same bed."

His eyes darkened as she continued to step closer to him until his back was up against his door, and she saw his hand inching closer to the doorknob. He turned it, and they both spilled into the room behind them. He shut the door and inched her back against it, leaning into her this time.

"And what is your defense?" he asked, his mouth inches from hers. "Do you have a list?"

"I … I do," she said hoarsely, her hands resting on his chest, stroking him through his waistcoat and linen shirt. Her fingers slipped lower, beginning to undo the buttons from his waist up. When she had succeeded, she slipped the coat off of his shoulders.

"First — we will stay much warmer if we are together."

"Agreed." He reached around her back and it was his turn to undo the long row of buttons.

"Second — the maids will only have to change one set of linens."

"That's an excellent point." As he pushed the dress off of her shoulders, he began to kiss the skin that appeared to him, and she shivered.

"Third — if … if I have a n-nightmare, you are close by."

"I wouldn't want to be far." He brushed his hand over her bosom and her head fell back. He took advantage and kissed her neck.

"Fourth — I … I've forgotten my list."

"Fourth," he continued, now divesting her of her gown, and she watched it pool in a pink froth on the floor. "We can spend our mornings together if we so choose, without having to dress first."

"Yes," she breathed, her fingers digging into his chest as she pulled at the buttons of his shirt with far less grace. "That is a good point."

"And fifth and finally — for I have always preferred lists in sets of five — I can do this—" he sucked on the bud of her nipple through her chemise, "—or this—" he ran a hand down her body to cup her womanhood, "—any time I like."

She couldn't say a thing any longer, but let out a squeak as he picked her up and carried her to the bed, somehow untying her stays and lifting her chemise overhead as he lay her down. She felt awkward for a moment, bare in front of him, but he began to strip off the rest of his own clothing and she soon forgot her embarrassment.

"My goodness," she said, staring, unable to take her eyes away from him. "Just what do you think you are going to do with *that*?"

He stopped, his eyes widening as he looked at her. "Do you not— this is, I realize that you are an innocent, of course, but are you not aware of the ... facts of what happens between man and woman?"

"Oh, I know," she said with flourish, "but somehow I simply do *not* think we are going to fit. How on earth do you walk around with that in your pants all day?"

He laughed then, a deep, hearty laugh that sent shivers through her body and yet oddly also allowed warmth to begin pooling in her stomach. She could listen to him laugh all day, she thought, before her mind returned to the task at hand, as it were.

"Who told you of activities of this nature?"

"Olivia," she said, her nose in the air as he crawled onto the bed over top of her.

"Well, it seems Olivia may have forgotten to mention a

few things. I do not blame her, with you being like a sister to her," he said, cocking his head at her. "How about this, Anne? You come here, kiss me, and we will see where things lead. If you decide that you do not want to go any further, then by all means, I shall stop. I always will, if you deem it. Now, does that work for you?"

"You do come up with the most-perfect plans," she said with a smile, the tension that had filled her body relaxing somewhat. "Now you will have to lead me through, step by step."

"Oh, you little minx," he said before he practically pounced on her, and she gave a shriek of delight as his hard body came over top her, propelling her back onto the bed, though he held himself up and off of her on his elbows. "I think," he whispered in her ear, "I've had enough of talking. How about instead of telling you, I show you?"

"I think I would be fine with that," she said, trying to maintain some composure, though she could barely think straight through her anticipation.

He started with a quick kiss on her lips, then moved up, to her nose and her forehead, before going back down and raining kisses over the side of her neck. He progressed down her chest, her stomach, then the insides of her thighs. Anne practically came off the bed. She had never felt anything so exquisite, yet positively thrilling at the same time.

"Christopher," she moaned, needing something from him, though what, she wasn't entirely sure. He seemed to know, however. His mouth found her nipples, giving them equal attention while his hand came to her center, cupping her, stroking her, and making her feel as though she was going to go out of her mind.

She lifted her hips to him as she took his face in her hands and brought it to her own, kissing him long and deep, showing him what she wanted, what she needed from him in turn.

He broke away for but a moment, whispering, "Are you ready?" and she nodded, steeling herself for what was to come. She felt him near her entrance, and she closed her eyes as she tried not to think of how big he was, how she really didn't see any way he was going to fit inside of her. Ever so slowly, he began to fill her, and she suddenly she forgot her fears and lifted her hips up to meet him.

"Ow!" she said into Christopher's shoulder, and he stroked her back gently with his fingers. "Just give it a minute, love," he said. "Let me know when you're ready again."

At first, she didn't think she would ever be — she thought this was actually a very bad idea. But then, the pain she felt slowly began to ebb away, and she was left with only wanting more of this, more of him, and she began to move against him of her own will. He looked down at her, and, clearly seeing the agreement on her face, he began to move with her in time.

Oh, this was better than anything she could have ever imagined, she thought. It felt … glorious. And then, Anne finally stopped thinking altogether, and let both her mind and body go free, to explore and enjoy the sensations that filled it.

"Christopher!" she shouted as she felt something growing inside of her, something that felt as though it were going to explode at any minute — and she could hardly wait for that moment.

"Come for me, Anne," he said, and she wasn't entirely sure what he meant by that, but then that feeling — the one he had caused within her before — came over her again, beginning in her middle and then exploding out through every part of her body. She didn't know if she shouted or not, but then Christopher was groaning her name and shuddering over top of her.

Before she knew it, he had collapsed down next to her and was pulling her close into his body, his head resting on top of hers.

"Christopher?" she said.

"Mm-hmm?"

"That was amazing."

"Yes, yes, it was."

"Oh, and Christopher?"

"Yes?"

"Do you think it *is* all right if we share the same bedroom?"

He laughed. "I think you have made your point very, very clear. I loved your list, but your practical, physical explanation was much better."

She laughed as well, then turned over and kissed him again, the kiss which promised forever.

EPILOGUE

"Very good, Bobby! Now, this time, make sure to enunciate your words."

"What does that mean, My Lady?"

"It means to say each and every syllable as clearly as you can. All right, now—"

"What's a syllable?"

Christopher smiled as he watched Anne's clearly forced smile while she tried to explain to the boy what a syllable was. He slipped back out of the theatre room and continued down the corridor to his office. Anne had decided that their stage needed to be shared. Not only was she directing a group of villagers, and even some nearby gentry — including in fact, one of the Ladies Winterton — in a play to be held later this month, but she had arranged a children's group to open up the night with a short play. Christopher wasn't sure if she found it more difficult to lead the children or the adults. Ella helped her and was actually starring in the next show.

He certainly wasn't getting involved, although he did enjoy checking in now and again to watch her in action. It was entertaining to be sure, but nothing was better than the times when he went in and she was alone, sitting at the pianoforte, her voice ringing out through the cavernous room. Christopher could hardly believe that at one point in time he had felt her voice should be muzzled, and not shared in its full glory for all to hear. It would have been a tragedy of his making. For she had a talent, unlike anything he had ever heard before. She could act as well, true, but her voice … it was unbelievable.

He was lost in his thoughts about her when his steward knocked on the door of his office, but when he saw the man, he waved him in, always appreciating the opportunity to review everything, ensure all was in order.

When his steward left, Christopher sensed someone in the room, and he looked up to see his wife. His smile grew as she walked toward him, and when he held out an arm to her, she promptly came over and took a seat on his lap.

"Hello, darling," she said, giving him a quick kiss on the lips. "Did you enjoy Bobby's performance?"

"How did you know I was there?"

She shrugged and rested her head on his shoulder. "Somehow, I just know when you are in the same room," she said. "Would you like to join next time?"

"Ha, not at all," he said with a snort of laughter. "Though I do enjoy watching you try to organize those rascals."

"They are not rascals!"

"What are they then?"

"They are … mischievous," she said. "I was much the same, I am told."

"Somehow, I believe it."

"Any*way*, Christopher, I wanted to speak with you about something. I was thinking of inviting a theatre group to come to play on our stage next month," she said. "What do you think of that?"

He looked at her with eyebrows raised, pausing as he considered her request.

"I suppose it would be wonderful for you and many of our neighbors," he said slowly. "Although this time, if you choose to join them, be sure to tell me first, all right?"

His heart quickened even as he said it. He pretended he was fine with her idea of eventually traveling, but in truth, he was far too worried for her safety. He had told her he wouldn't hold her back, however, and he had to be true to his word.

She surprised him by laughing, and he let out the breath he hadn't even known he was holding.

"Oh, Christopher," she said. "I could never leave you, not again. I am perfectly happy performing right here and sharing my love of the theatre with others nearby. Besides, it would not be seemly for me to be traveling about the country, in my condition and all."

"Your condition?"

"Yes," she said with a glint in her eye, "no one wants to see an expectant woman onstage."

Christopher let out a whoop so very unlike him and lifted her high in the air, twirling her around before stopping suddenly and setting her back on her feet.

"I suppose I shouldn't do such things."

"Don't be silly," she said, putting her hand on his arm. "It is very early yet. Are you ready, Christopher, truly? For nothing will change our lives more than a child. Or a little rascal, as you say."

"I would want nothing more," he said, popping a kiss on her nose. "Even if they are as much trouble as you are."

"Your life would be very boring without a little trouble in it."

"So I am told," he grinned. "And you know what, Anne? I wouldn't want it any other way."

***

Dear reader,

I hope you enjoyed reading Anne and Christopher's story! If you have read through the entire Happily Ever After series, I hope it has brought you a great deal of joy and love.

If you love strong, independent women and men who love them, you will also enjoy Quest of Honor! It is the first book in my Searching Hearts series, featuring the sons and daughters of a duke. Start with Thomas, the wayward son who longs for freedom from his privileged life and falls for the wrong woman in the enemies-to-lovers adventure you can find here.

If you haven't yet signed up for my newsletter, I would love to have you join us! You will receive a free book, as well as links to giveaways, sales, new releases, and stories about my coffee addiction, my struggle to keep my plants alive, and how much trouble one loveable wolf-lookalike dog can get into.

www.elliestclair.com/ellies-newsletter

Or you can join my Facebook group, Ellie St. Clair's Ever Afters, and stay in touch daily.

Until next time, happy reading!

With love,

Ellie

* * *

Quest of Honor
Searching Hearts Book One

* * *

HE LONGS FOR FREEDOM, but when he catches Eleanor Adams, he gets far more than he bargained for...

Thomas Harrington, second son of the Duke of Ware, joined the Royal Navy to escape from his life in society and find the freedom his soul had been searching for. Instead, he has spent three years attempting to bring the elusive pirate Captain Adams to justice.

Eleanor has only known life on the high seas with her gentleman pirate captain of her father, evading the naval captain who refuses to give up his relentless pursuit – unless he can discover a way to capture him instead.

The beautiful blonde woman Thomas meets in a tavern haunts his dreams, until he finds her in the unlikeliest of circumstances. The freedom his soul has been searching for and the honor he so upholds clash within him as Thomas and Eleanor fight their desire for one another. As they question everything they've ever believed, can they find a way forward together?

AN EXCERPT FROM QUEST OF HONOR

⁂

"I'd say he looks quite miserable," Eleanor whispered, clenching her fists in her skirts, "and I am glad of it."

"We should return to the ship," the first mate warned. "It is some miles away and, now that we know he is here, your father will wish to weigh anchor immediately."

Eleanor knew he was right. Their trip to Port Royal had been a successful one, bartering for more goods and ensuring that they had enough food for their next adventure, but it was always intertwined with danger. Now that the British were attempting to "clean up" Port Royal, they had been forced to be much more careful. However, the port was large and the *Gunsway* had been anchored a few miles off shore with flags lowered so that they could not be easily identified. Besides that, they were only one of many ships near Port Royal, and, as soon as it began to grow dark, Eleanor knew her father intended to leave and return to open water.

She and Morgan were securing the final goods in town and had stopped at the tavern. It was there that Morgan had pointed out Captain Harrington sitting at the bar, alone. Eleanor knew the best course of action was to leave as soon as possible to warn her father, but she couldn't help but be intrigued. His name had hung over her head for three years now, yet she had never seen him herself.

Now, watching him sit there, morose and alone, he seemed just an ordinary man. One who, at the moment, seemed defeated. Perhaps... perhaps this wasn't a risk, but an opportunity.

"I'm going to speak to him," she said, standing abruptly.

"No, Adams," hissed the first mate, referring to her as he had always done, "you cannot."

Eleanor frowned. "Why not? I am in skirts, am I not?" In truth, she much preferred breeches, but she drew too much attention when she wore her usual garb on shore. It was better that, on this particular visit, they stay hidden. "He will believe me to work here." In one capacity or another.

"Why would you speak to him?" Morgan whispered, hoarsely. "There is no need, Adams. We already know who he is!"

"Because I wish to look him in the eye," Eleanor replied, fiercely. "I would stare into the face of my enemy, unafraid." She paused, losing her ire as practicality reigned. "Besides that, he appears to be in his cups and may have some worthwhile information for us. I will meet you back at the ship."

Eleanor's rank on the ship was an undefined one. The crew respected her and considered her one of their own. Her father had made known his intentions for her to succeed him one day, but at the moment, she held no type of rank at all. She didn't give orders, but she also did not follow every order given by the first mate — at least, not in decisions off the ship. Without giving him a chance to argue, she pushed away from the table and walked over to the barman, requesting another whisky for Captain Harrington.

"You're with him, are you?" the barman grunted, looking her up and down as though she were one of the easy women who worked around Port Royal. She wished she could invoke the Adams name, but the fewer people who knew her identity here, the better. "Well, at least you're cleaner than the other ones who come here."

Eleanor bit back her harsh retort, managing a hard smile as the barman handed her the whisky. Picking it up, she walked over to the captain, her heartbeat increasing as it did when a battle loomed as she approached him.

"Did I hear the barman say you are a captain?" she asked smoothly, sitting down opposite him without invitation.

A pair of eyes the color of shallow waters looked up at her warily. "I did not think His Majesty's Navy was much admired in these parts."

Eleanor pretended to be upset and pouted. "I was merely bringing you another whisky, sir," she replied quietly, lowering her eyelids. "I am sorry if that was the wrong thing to do. You simply look a little unhappy. I thought I might change that."

The hard expression dimmed as he raised his eyebrows at her and, to Eleanor's shock and dismay, she realized that he was quite a handsome man. She told herself the surge of attraction to him was nothing more than a physical urge as she kept the smile on her face while he sat back and studied her with those cool blue eyes framed by chiseled cheekbones.

His jaw tightened as his eyes wandered over from her face, over her shoulders upon which her hair hung loose, down her figure, pausing where she knew her breasts were swelling over the neckline of her blouse, though not as suggestively as most of the barmaids. His countenance changed, and he smiled at her, surprising her with his crooked grin, a dimple etched into one cheek.

He ran a hand through his straight dark hair as it fell

from its tie, and her fingers itched to run through its silkiness. She clenched them into fists.

This is your enemy, Eleanor, she reminded herself, *you feel nothing but hatred.*

"I should not have been so harsh," he murmured, reaching for what was now his fifth whisky, at least by her count since she had begun watching him. "My temper quite gets the better of me at times, particularly in days of late. Now tell me, what has brought a woman as beautiful as you to a place like this?"

"The same thing that brings us all here in one way or another," she replied with a coy smile of her own. "Pirate treasure."

He chuckled ruefully, shaking his head. "Most of it is said to be gone. The glory days of the pirates are over. If you are seeking out those clinging to the days of old, why choose this table, then? You must know an officer of the Royal Navy is not the place to find your treasure."

"You looked so lost over here by yourself," she replied, with what she hoped was a look of pity. "I thought you could use another drink — and some company."

"Your presence is welcome," he replied, leaning in and twirling a lock of her hair around his index finger. "I must admit, I am rather lonely."

Eleanor said nothing, the rising hairs at the back of her neck warning her that this had been as bad of an idea as Morgan had warned her. She had to leave—now. If she stayed, she would have no choice but to follow through on this charade she had begun.

"Excuse me, sir," she said, getting up from the table as gracefully as she could. "There are other customers."

His hand shot out and strong, calloused fingers wrapped around hers, keeping her close. "The barman will not mind, I am sure," he said, firmly. Eleanor saw him lift his head and catch the barman's eye, who, to her horror, simply chuckled and tipped his head toward one of the doors to his left.

This was all going disastrously wrong. A surge of fire swept through Eleanor as she forced herself to sit back down. She must behave as any other woman might, not the woman she truly was. The woman she was playing to be would be eager to accept the captain's attention.

"Can I get you another whisky, sir?" she asked, hoping that this might be a way to make her escape.

"No, I think not," Harrington murmured, throwing back the remains of his glass before trying to stand. He swayed slightly, as even a man of his size had knocked back quite a few glasses in a short space of time. "I have not enjoyed a woman's company for a long while now. I am not normally a man who pays for a good time, but there's a spark to you – you speak to me. Perhaps you're just what I need to clear my head and lift my spirits."

Eleanor felt her stomach tighten as he wrapped a strong arm around her waist and led her away from the table. She turned around looking for Morgan, but he had disappeared, likely to finish their business of the day. She was no innocent young woman, but this was her *enemy*, the man who wanted to see her father hanged. She had to be smart. If she ran now, he would only become far too suspicious, and if he followed her, she would be putting her father and the crew at far greater risk than they would have been from the start. Why had she not listened to Morgan and left the man alone?

The worst part of it all was that Eleanor had to admit to herself that she was not completely opposed to the idea of going to bed with this man. Strong muscles revealed themselves through his shirt, and his drunken clumsiness was lending somewhat of a charm to his bearing. She felt like a traitor as her body and mind struggled over how to respond to the British captain.

"Top of the stairs to your left," the barman grinned, as Harrington slammed down some money on top of the bar. "Thank you, sir. Most generous."

He's paying for my services, Eleanor realized, going cold all over. She tried to breathe slowly as he stumbled up the stairs, her mind working furiously. Maybe she would be able to knock him out somehow, and then make her escape.

"What is it that you need relief from, sir?" she asked, hating that her voice trembled a little. "Perhaps I can help you in other ways."

He snorted, pushing the door open slightly too hard so that it banged loudly against the next wall. "Unless you can find Captain Adams, my dear girl, then I do not think you can relieve my true torment."

"Ah, so you are hunting a pirate," she trilled, leaning in and running a hand down his chest as though she was comforting him. "If he is causing you so much difficulty, then why do you not simply give up? I am sure the Navy will find much better things for you to do. After all, he is only one pirate and there are so many around Port Royal. You could take your pick."

Throwing his hat and coat onto the chair in the corner of the room, the captain faced her, his face ravaged. The change in his demeanor shocked her, although she kept her features schooled into a sympathetic smile.

"I dream of freedom," he rasped, stepping closer and grasping her arms with strong hands, as if willing her to feel his desperation. "I can have none until I catch him. The Royal Navy does not accept failure."

"Must you stay in the Navy?" she asked, reaching a hand and running it over his hair as she had yearned to do earlier. "Have you no other options?"

"Not if I am to keep my family from dishonor."

"Leaving the Navy would cause this?"

"They were shocked when I joined the Navy. Now I have spent three years in a search of one man. I am a laughing-stock, but if I find him, bring him to justice — well then, perhaps, I will have restored the honor I lost and can find a new path."

Eleanor looked up into his eyes, finding them cold but haunted — and in that moment, something shifted within her. "You're trapped."

"Trapped," he nodded, as if musing over the word, "that is exactly what I am."

"Despite travelling the world over the open seas."

"I'd prefer to see the world on my own terms," he replied, a faraway look in his eye. "However, I have seen more than I would have ever thought possible. Even this town, as dirty as it is, has beaches that are something to behold, and the palm trees and crystal-blue ocean are simply… magnificent."

"No, I do not suppose they have beaches such as these where you are from," she replied with a smile, thinking of the rocky caves where they stored their treasure. "Where will you go next?"

"I'll follow the pirate until the day I catch up to him. I should hope that day comes sooner rather than later." Tipping his head, his eyes blazed into hers as he ran his hands lightly down her arms, catching her hands. He unconsciously stroked her wrists, sending tingles through her body. "Over and over I search for him, and always come up short."

"Perhaps you are not meant to capture this particular pirate," she murmured, which stilled the stroke of his fingers.

"Why this sudden care for Captain Adams?" he asked, eyeing her warily from somewhat glassy eyes. "Do you know the man?"

She let out what she hoped was a carefree laugh.

"The fabled pirate Captain Adams? I could only wish. As

I'm sure you know, Captain, he does not frequent such establishments as this. I'm afraid you will have to continue your search for Captain Adams — and your freedom — elsewhere."

"That I will. In the meantime, perhaps you can help me remember what freedom tastes like."

Find out what happens next in Quest of Honor!

ALSO BY ELLIE ST. CLAIR

Happily Ever After
The Duke She Wished For
Someday Her Duke Will Come
Once Upon a Duke's Dream
He's a Duke, But I Love Him
Loved by the Viscount
Because the Earl Loved Me

Happily Ever After Box Set Books 1-3
Happily Ever After Box Set Books 4-6

Reckless Rogues
The Earls's Secret
The Viscount's Code
Prequel, The Duke's Treasure, available in:
I Like Big Dukes and I Cannot Lie

The Remingtons of the Regency
The Mystery of the Debonair Duke
The Secret of the Dashing Detective
The Clue of the Brilliant Bastard
The Quest of the Reclusive Rogue

The Unconventional Ladies
Lady of Mystery
Lady of Fortune

Lady of Providence

Lady of Charade

The Unconventional Ladies Box Set

To the Time of the Highlanders

A Time to Wed

A Time to Love

A Time to Dream

Thieves of Desire

The Art of Stealing a Duke's Heart

A Jewel for the Taking

A Prize Worth Fighting For

Gambling for the Lost Lord's Love

Romance of a Robbery

Thieves of Desire Box Set

The Bluestocking Scandals

Designs on a Duke

Inventing the Viscount

Discovering the Baron

The Valet Experiment

Writing the Rake

Risking the Detective

A Noble Excavation

A Gentleman of Mystery

The Bluestocking Scandals Box Set: Books 1-4

The Bluestocking Scandals Box Set: Books 5-8

Blooming Brides

A Duke for Daisy

A Marquess for Marigold

An Earl for Iris

A Viscount for Violet

The Blooming Brides Box Set: Books 1-4

The Victorian Highlanders

Duncan's Christmas - (prequel)

Callum's Vow

Finlay's Duty

Adam's Call

Roderick's Purpose

Peggy's Love

The Victorian Highlanders Box Set Books 1-5

Searching Hearts

Duke of Christmas (prequel)

Quest of Honor

Clue of Affection

Hearts of Trust

Hope of Romance

Promise of Redemption

Searching Hearts Box Set (Books 1-5)

Christmas

Christmastide with His Countess

Her Christmas Wish

Merry Misrule
A Match Made at Christmas
A Match Made in Winter

Standalones

Always Your Love
The Stormswept Stowaway
A Touch of Temptation

For a full list of all of Ellie's books, please see www.elliestclair.com/books.

ABOUT THE AUTHOR

Ellie has always loved reading, writing, and history. For many years she has written short stories, non-fiction, and has worked on her true love and passion -- romance novels.

In every era there is the chance for romance, and Ellie enjoys exploring many different time periods, cultures, and geographic locations. No matter when or where, love can always prevail. She has a particular soft spot for the bad boys of history, and loves a strong heroine in her stories.

Ellie and her husband love nothing more than spending time at home with their children and Husky cross. Ellie can typically be found at the lake in the summer, pushing the stroller all year round, and, of course, with her computer in her lap or a book in hand.

She also loves corresponding with readers, so be sure to contact her!

www.elliestclair.com
ellie@elliestclair.com

- facebook.com/elliestclairauthor
- twitter.com/ellie_stclair
- instagram.com/elliestclairauthor
- amazon.com/author/elliestclair
- goodreads.com/elliestclair
- bookbub.com/authors/elliest.clair
- pinterest.com/elliestclair

Printed by Amazon Italia Logistica S.r.l.
Torrazza Piemonte (TO), Italy